FINDING BLACK BEAUTY

Lou Kuenzler

Scholastic Children's Books
An imprint of Scholastic Ltd
Euston House, 24 Eversholt Street, London, NW1 1DB, UK
Registered office: Westfield Road, Southam, Warwickshire, CV47 0RA
SCHOLASTIC and associated logos are trademarks and/or
registered trademarks of Scholastic Inc.

First published in the UK by Scholastic Ltd, 2016
This edition published in 2017

ISBN 978 1407 18141 7

A CIP catalogue record for this book
is available from the British Library.

Printed by CPI Group (UK) Ltd, Croydon, CR0 4YY
Papers used by Scholastic Children's Books are made
from wood grown in sustainable forests.

1 3 5 7 9 10 8 6 4 2

www.scholastic.co.uk

ᴗᴗᴗ

To Mum and Dad for all my fond memories
of the real Summer's Place. LK

*"Poor Joe! He was young and small,
and as yet he knew very little..."*

Black Beauty *by Anna Sewell (1877)*

Part One
Summer's Place

Chapter One

The last time I saw Father, he was standing in the doorway at Summer's Place, wearing his scarlet hunting coat.

"Don't go! Why can't you just leave the poor fox alone?" I said.

"Josephine Judith Green, I never knew you were so soft-hearted," he sighed.

"I'm not soft-hearted," I said.

Nanny Clay snorted with laughter on the stairs behind me. "Begging your pardon, sir. You could describe your daughter as many things ... but soft-hearted isn't one of them," she said. "Stubborn maybe. Or spoilt. Or rude. Or..."

"I'm sure you're right!" Father gave Nanny Clay

a little bow. She was his nanny too when he was a boy. Neither of us are ever brave enough to argue with her properly – not even Father, though he's a grown-up and Lord of the Manor with the finest horses in all the county. "Josie might be jolly rude to people," he teased, "but she is daft as a duckling when it comes to animals."

"I'm not a duckling. I just feel sorry for the poor fox!" I thumped my fists against the banister as I heard the hounds baying in the paddock outside.

"Watch your temper, young lady!" warned Nanny Clay.

But Father just smiled.

"I'm sure you would feel differently if you came hunting with me," he said, stepping out the door.

"Oh, may I?" I leapt down the last stairs in a single bound, almost tripping over the hem of my frock. "Thomas could have Merrylegs saddled in five minutes flat."

All thoughts of the poor fox vanished from my mind like a snuffed-out candle. All I could think about was leaping ditches, crouching flat on Merrylegs's neck as we thundered over the fields with the hunt.

"We'll keep up with the pack," I promised.

"I know Merrylegs is small and tubby and I've outgrown him . . . but we'll gallop like the wind."

"I'm sure you would." Father shook his head. "But I'm sorry, Josie – you can't come. I was only teasing. You know I promised your mother I would never let you hunt. She always said it was too dangerous."

"Why? What does she care what I do – she isn't here to stop me!" Mother left us when I was a baby and never came back; it was still the talk of the county after all these years. "You don't care what I do either, Father," I cried. "You care more for your fancy new hunter than you do for me."

I saw a look of hurt come into his eyes and he took a step back.

"Enough, young madam!" Nanny Clay shook her finger. "There is no call to speak to your poor papa like that. Him, who has done his best to raise you on his own ever since your flighty mother danced off to London without so much as a backwards glance."

"Keep Mother out of this!" I snapped. It broke my heart that she had left, but I hated the way other people always tried to blame her.

"I'm sorry, Josie." Father turned towards the door. "The subject is closed. But you're right about one

3

thing. Little Merrylegs is too small for you now. I'll talk to Thomas. We'll find you a nice quiet mare."

"I don't want a silly mare. I don't want anything. Go off and kill your fox. I hate you!" I spat.

Of course, I wish I had never said it now.

I wish I had told him to be careful.

I wish I had told him I loved him.

But I never got the chance.

They carried Father's body into the house on a plank of wood. I couldn't see his face; it was covered with his scarlet hunting jacket. There was a dark stain all down one side, darker than the bright red coat.

I screamed. But I couldn't cry. It was as if everything was in a fog.

I knew Father's broken body was underneath that coat. But I couldn't bear to think about him being dead. All I could think was how strange it was to see old Thomas the groom and his stable lad inside the house. I had only ever seen them outside or in the stables. They put him carefully on the floor and someone – Thomas, I think – told me a doctor had been sent for. But I knew it was too late, there was no saving him.

"Sir Charles was dead the minute he hit the

ground," I heard Thomas murmur quietly to the stable lad. "First time out on the new hunter and he took the ditch too fast. Never felt a thing, I shouldn't think."

The fog in my brain got thicker.

"Mind you go out through the servants' hall," I told them sharply. Somebody had to take charge — that was my job now.

"Yes, Miss . . . and our condolences." Old Thomas bowed, his cap bunched up in his hands. "Come on, lad."

The stable boy — I had forgotten his name — gave me a nod, and then they both left.

Nanny Clay laid a hand on my arm.

"You poor child," she sobbed. Tears were streaming down her plump pink apple cheeks. "Come away while the doctor does his work."

I shook off her attempts at comfort.

"No. I will stay with Father — it is my duty," I said, trying to sound firm even though my knees were shaking and my voice was little more than a whisper. "I am mistress of Summer's Place now."

But I was wrong about that. By the time Father was buried in the family plot in our little church beyond the meadow, his lawyer, Mr Hadaway, had come to read the will. "I'm not sure how much your father told you about how the estate was left, my dear," he said, and I shook my head. "It is customary," he explained, "for inheritance to avoid the female line."

"What does that mean?" I asked, staring at him. "That I get nothing, because I'm a girl?"

"Not nothing," said Mr Hadaway quickly. "When you marry you will receive an allowance."

"But I'm only twelve. I won't get married for years. . ." None of this made any sense. My head was spinning. "Who will own Summer's Place? The land? The horses?"

Mr Hadaway coughed. "Your – ah – second cousin Eustace has been named heir," he said.

"Eustace?" I couldn't bear it. The last time Eustace had been here all he had done was pull my hair and bully the kitchen cat. "He is greedy. He is lazy. And he cannot even ride!" I cried.

"Have a care. That is the new master of Summer's Place you are talking about," said Mr Hadaway.

But I was already running across the hall and out of the door towards the stable yard.

"Oh, Merrylegs," I sobbed, dashing into his stall

and flinging my arms around the tubby pony's dappled neck. "Everything is ruined now."

I clutched his shaggy grey mane, crying properly for the first time since Father died. I was dry-eyed at the funeral (even though Nanny Clay stowed three handkerchiefs in the cuffs of my black dress and sobbed her way through at least eight hankies of her own).

But now I wept big gulping tears that would not stop. Nanny Clay was right; Father had spoiled me dreadfully. But he had teased me too; he had loved me, and he had taught me to ride. I had loved him and now he was gone. I cried for the loss of my proud, funny father.

And I cried for me.

"Oh, Merrylegs," I wailed. "Nothing will ever be the same again."

Chapter Two

Cousin Eustace had been at Summer's Place for three weeks before I saw him step outside.

It was such a waste! He was only six months older than me. There were at least a dozen horses in the stables eager for exercise. The land agent came every day asking the "young master" to ride the boundaries and see the land. But Eustace just shut himself away in the drawing room with a pair of little clippers, growing mustard and cress plants in the scooped-out shells of boiled eggs.

"Like hair for Humpty Dumpty," as Nanny Clay said.

"Country air is such a challenge for him," his mother, my Aunt Lavinia, explained to us one morning. "The dear, delicate boy has such a sensitive soul. He is quite unused to wind and weather and the smell of farmyard dung."

"Indeed, Mother." Eustace blinked, sipping a glass of milk as pale as his pasty skin, which never saw the light of day.

"If you don't like it here, go back to London," I said. "Leave me in charge. At the very least you should ride out and meet the tenants. It is your duty. . ."

"You would be well advised to mind your own affairs, Josephine," Aunt Lavinia scolded. "Eustace is master of Summer's Place now and, until he comes of age, I shall act as mistress of the Manor, offering support and guidance to the dear boy."

"But Father rode every day," I said.

"I think we are all aware of your father's obsession with horses." Aunt Lavinia peered over her spectacles. "To follow the example of a man who galloped into his own grave seems most misguided to me."

"Misguided indeed." Eustace giggled as he slurped his milk.

"How dare you!" I cried, tears prickling my eyes. "Everything you have here – everything at Summer's

Place – is thanks to Father . . . and his father before him."

"Well, there will be changes now. I have plans." Aunt Lavinia lifted a small gold notebook and pencil from the table. She was forever writing lists in it, and made such a show of scribbling and sighing, I knew she wanted me to ask what they were about. But I wouldn't give her the satisfaction. I turned on my heel and walked calmly to the door.

"I have plans of my own," I said.

"Really?" sneered Aunt Lavinia. "Well, enjoy them while you can."

As soon as I was out of the room, I gathered up my skirts and ran.

"Nanny Clay," I cried, almost bumping into her as I charged into the nursery. "Tell the stable lad to saddle Merrylegs. I shall be going for a ride."

"But you're still in mourning for your father." Nanny Clay looked shocked.

"Yes! And I have been cooped up far too long already," I raged, kicking at the skirting board. "If I stay inside another moment I shall become as pale and useless as The Slug."

"That is no way to talk about your Cousin Eustace—"

"Ha! But you knew who I meant. He is a slug. A lazy, hide-at-home nonsense of a boy. Him? Master of Summer's Place? Ugh. I wish I was a boy. If I was a boy, I would—"

"But you are not a boy," said Nanny Clay. "And *ifs* and *wishes* will break your heart. I should know. I have been told today that I must—"

"I tell you what is *worse* than a slug!" I cut across her. "A scorpion! That's what Aunt Lavinia is with all her nasty notes and little plans. A scorpion with a sting in her tail."

"You may be right." Nanny Clay sighed. "But I don't suppose it is fitting for a young lady to say so."

"I don't care what's fitting." I groaned. "I don't care about mourning. Father is dead – wearing stupid tight-laced clothes and sipping tea will never bring him back. He's gone. And he wouldn't want me stuck inside like a butterfly in a cage."

"You? A butterfly? I've heard it all now." Nanny Clay began to giggle. "But you're right, Master Charlie . . . I mean Sir Charles, your father, God rest his soul – would want you out there enjoying the fresh air. I'll send word to the stables to have the pony saddled."

"You'll need to put my hair up and tell the maid to bring my riding clothes as well," I said.

"Yes, Your Majesty!" Nanny Clay gave a great exaggerated curtsy as if I was a queen. She bobbed down so low I heard her old knees creak. "At least your riding habit is black and your hat has a veil. That shows some respect, at least."

Five minutes later she was brushing out my long red hair.

"Ninety-four, ninety-five..." She battled with a knot behind my ear.

"Ouch!" I yelped as my head wrenched back, but Nanny Clay barely missed a beat.

"... Ninety-seven... It was like rats' tails when I started, but see now... Like burnished copper. You look more like your mother every day," she said.

"No!" Was Nanny Clay teasing? My mother was a beauty. I turned and looked at the portrait hanging on the nursery wall behind us. Father had paid a famous artist to paint Mother when they were first married ... just after she gave up being an actress on the London stage. A little brass plate underneath the picture said: *Lady Valentina Green, 1863*.

"Your father had that painting moved up here

into your nursery the day she ran away," said Nanny Clay, seeing me looking at it. She had told me the story a hundred times before. But I liked hearing it – there was so little I really knew of Mother. "He said you should always have it by you. A young girl needs her mama watching over her. But he never wanted to set eyes on it again."

I stared at the painting.

"Do you really think I look like her?" I felt a hot blush creep up my neck. It couldn't be true. Mother was perfect, like a goddess. That's why she ran away. She was too special . . . too golden to stay stuck here in the country with us. Surely I looked nothing like her – not with my carrot-orange hair and freckled nose.

"Hmm!" Nanny Clay turned her back on the portrait. "Fine looks are for the rainbow," she said. "It's fine morals that keep folk on the ground. Just remember that when I'm not here to guide you. . ."

"But you'll always be here, Nanny Clay." I laughed. "You are as much a part of Summer's Place as the stable clock."

"Tick-tock, times change." She sighed.

Before I could ask what she meant, her mouth was full of pins and she was tugging my long loose hair into a bun.

Chapter Three

I dashed into the stable yard, desperate to be off on Merrylegs, out in the fresh air. I expected him to be waiting for me by the mounting block but there was no sign of him.

"What's taking so long?" I sighed. I was about to call out, when I heard old Thomas the groom talking to the stable lad in the stalls. I still couldn't remember the boy's name.

Something made me stop and listen. Their voices were hushed and hurried as if they were sharing secrets ... but the stony walls made their words echo like a well.

"... This new lot don't care for horses," whispered the boy.

"At least you're young," said old Thomas. "I hear they're looking for lads up at Birtwick Park. Nice estate, the other side of the Beacon Hills. Squire Gordon keeps a fine stable."

"If it's so fine, why are they missing a lad?" the boy asked.

"The last one's gone off to be a soldier." Thomas coughed hard – he's been wheezing for years now because of the dust in the hay.

"Smart fellow. Reckon I might do the same. This job's a thankless one and no mistake," grumbled the boy.

"Not tired of the horses, are you?" asked Thomas.

"Of course not," said the lad. I heard the echoey sound of him patting Merrylegs's neck. "It's them up in the big house I can't be doing with."

Ha! Even the servants agreed with me! Who'd want to work for Aunt Lavinia and The Slug.

But what the stable lad said next made my cheeks burn with shame.

"Gentry!" he snorted. "No manners at all. They're too la-di-da to take sugar without a silver spoon, but I bet half of them don't even know my name."

"Ha! You'd be right there, young Billy," Thomas said with a wheeze.

"Billy!" I whispered, burying my head in my hands. Of course! I remembered now.

"The master was different though," I heard Thomas say. "He knew every lad on this estate."

For a moment I felt a pang of real shame. Then I shook my head. This was ridiculous. What did it matter if I knew the boy's name or not? How was I supposed to keep track of every servant we ever employed?

"Are you going to gossip in there all day?" I called. "Because I should like to ride some time today."

There was a shocked silence in the stable. Then Billy emerged, his cheeks as red as mine.

"Sorry to keep you waiting," he mumbled, as he led Merrylegs to the mounting block. "Only we didn't know you were here."

"Clearly," I snapped. Embarrassment and fury were wrestling inside me. Fury won. "I've never waited so long for a ride in all my life."

I wish now that I had smiled at him instead. I wish I had said: "Thank you, Billy. There's no real hurry at all." But I did not.

I turned my back on him and Thomas helped me mount.

"Comfortable, Miss Josephine?" he asked as soon as I was seated side-saddle.

"Yes, thank you." Merrylegs was fidgeting, dancing from foot to foot and throwing his little head in the air. He was too small to be exercised by anyone but me and hadn't been ridden since Father died.

"I'll go past the dairy, over the winter pasture and up along the side of Sewell's Farm," I told Thomas. Father and I had always had a pact that I could ride alone so long as I told Thomas where I was going, and it felt good to honour that now he was gone.

"Right you are, Miss Josephine." He laughed as Merrylegs tossed his head. "He's keen to be off," he said. "Make the most of it, Miss Josephine. Enjoy the little fellow, while you still can."

That seemed an odd thing to say, but before I could question Thomas, Merrylegs had bounded forward like a hare in a meadow, and we were off.

The minute Merrylegs and I were past the dairy and out of sight of the stable yard, I wriggled in the side-saddle and threw one leg over his back so that I was riding astride.

"That's better!" I cried, digging both heels in as he galloped flat out across the short-cropped pasture. His long grey mane whipped me in the face, blown up by the chilly wind. It was the first day of March, and still cold; but while I had been shut away indoors, spring had come. The hedgerows were full of buds and furled green leaves. Primroses speckled the grass.

"Beautiful!" I smiled, leaning low over Merrylegs's strong arched neck as they flashed past beneath me.

As we reached the edge of Sewell's Farm, I slowed to a trot but I didn't swing my leg back over to side-saddle again. I could see the farmer leaning on his gate and rode over to say hello. We often saw each other on my rides and he was the only one who knew I secretly rode like a boy.

"Well, well, well. If it's not young Master Joseph from the big house." He chuckled. We shared the same joke every time.

"Greetings, Farmer Sewell." I stuck my elbows out and scratched my chin like I thought a boy might do.

"Strapping lad like you," teased the farmer, "I'm surprised you haven't run away to sea."

"Off tomorrow," I answered, looking back over my shoulder as Merrylegs and I dropped down on to the lane."Off to join a pirate ship. Aye aye."

"Best of luck to you, laddie," called the farmer and we both laughed just like we always did.

*

By the time I trotted back to the stable yard, I was seated side-saddle again, the picture of a fine young lady out for a gentle hack.

Good thing too; I was shocked to see Aunt Lavinia and The Slug outside.

Old Thomas was beside them, and Aunt Lavinia was pointing at the stable clock.

"That will have to go too," she said, scribbling in her little gold book. "The whole thing will have to come down."

"What are you talking about?" I cried, pulling on Merrylegs's reins as he stretched his head to sniff her hat. "You can't take down the stable clock."

"Why not?" Aunt Lavinia looked over at me with a nasty sour little grin as if she had sucked a lime. "We'll have no need for a stable clock if we have no stables."

"No stables?" I gasped.

"We're pulling them down," said Aunt Lavinia.

"And building a glass house for my plants," snuffled Eustace, shielding his eyes from the pale spring sun.

"Your plants?" I said. "Your cress seeds?" Surely egg shells didn't need a whole glass house of their own?

"There'll be ferns as well. And succulents." Eustace rubbed his hands. "All the fine estates have glass houses."

"But ... where will the horses live?" I asked. A tight pain was building in my chest. "Can't you keep the stables here and build your glass house by the lake?"

"Certainly not! Eustace cannot be expected to trail across the gardens just to look at plants. This is much the best site, right here beside the house. He'll barely need to go outside at all." Aunt Lavinia's smile was now as broad as the Cheshire Cat in my Alice in Wonderland book. "We'll have no need for stables. Not since all the horses are to be sold."

"Sold?" I almost choked on the word.

Out of the corner of my eye, I saw old Thomas stretch out his hand and steady himself against the stable wall.

"Yes. All of them," said Aunt Lavinia sharply. "We'll keep the matching bays to pull the carriage, of course... And that's it."

Chapter Four

The stables emptied day by day. I couldn't bear to watch the horses leave. But at least Merrylegs could stay, surely.

He was small enough to live in the old sheep barn in the meadow. He wouldn't even need a stable. There was no reason for Aunt Lavinia to get rid of him.

The very first horse to be sold was Magnum, the young hunter Father had been riding the day he died. Payment was sent by a breeder in Southampton and Billy was to ride him to the coast.

"I'll not be back," he told Nanny Clay, handing her a bundle of outgrown clothes to pass on to the poor children of the parish. "Reckon I'll head to the docks. See if there's a ship in need of a handy lad like me."

So he's the one who gets to run away to sea like a pirate, I thought. *He'll watch the sun set over Rio de Janeiro, while I rot indoors doing needlepoint with Aunt Lavinia and The Slug.* Her latest idea was that I should practise embroidery by sewing Eustace's initials on a set of table napkins.

"It is only fitting the new master of Summer's Place should have fresh linens." She smiled as I pricked my finger on the needle for the hundredth time.

As yet more horses were sold, I began to worry about Merrylegs.

"Aunt Lavinia?" I ventured one morning at breakfast. "Shall I instruct Thomas to put a hay rack in the old sheep barn? It will make a fine, dry shelter for Merrylegs once the stables are knocked down."

"Merry-who?" Aunt Lavinia blinked.

"Her fat pony." Eustace dipped a soldier of bread into his runny egg.

"Merrylegs isn't fat, he's just well-padded," I cried. "He has Welsh pony in him. He is a hardy breed."

"Then I am sure he will make the children at Birtwick a steady ride," said Aunt Lavinia, clicking her fingers for the footman to pull back her chair.

"But – but you can't sell Merrylegs!" I jumped up so quick my own chair toppled backwards. "He's mine. Father promised he could stay at Summer's Place for the rest of his life."

"Your father is no longer with us and I thought I made it quite clear there would be no more horses," Aunt Lavinia said.

"Merrylegs isn't a horse. He's a pony." My throat was so tight I could barely speak. "I never thought you meant to get rid of him as well." My hands were shaking so hard I knocked over my coffee cup.

"Honestly, Josephine. There is no need to create such a scene – all for a silly pony." Aunt Lavinia fluttered her grey silk fan.

I saw Eustace smirk as he sliced the top off his second boiled egg. That did it. I lunged forward, grabbed it from his eggcup and hurled it hard at Aunt Lavinia.

"Ouch!" She gasped as it hit her on the nose.

"Now you've done it," snorted Eustace, staring in horror as bright yellow yolk ran down Aunt Lavinia's chin.

But I wasn't finished. Before he could say another word, I grabbed the jug of milk and upturned it over

Eustace's head for good measure.

"Serves you both right," I cried, running for the door. "You have *ruined* Summer's Place."

"Get out! Vile brat," ordered Aunt Lavinia. "I forbid you to leave the nursery until church tomorrow morning."

"Good! I'll stay up there for ever. I don't care if I never see you again." I stormed out, leaving my aunt and cousin mopping their faces with their table napkins – the ones which still proudly bore my father's crest in green and gold.

I paced up and down the schoolroom, still trembling with rage.

"Pride! That's your problem," said Nanny Clay, wagging her finger.

"Oh please, don't scold me. Not today." I couldn't bear for her to be cross. I stared out of the window, watching a shower of rain patter against the glass. "I can't believe she's selling Merrylegs," I choked.

Nanny Clay raised herself up from her chair. I heard her stiff black mourning dress rustle like the feathers of a fighting cockerel.

Now I'm in for a lecture, I thought, pressing my forehead against the cool glass. But instead of scolding me, Nanny Clay laid her hand gently on my back.

"I know you love that old pony. I'm fond of the little fellow myself." She sighed. "But he's a thing of childhood. You'll have to leave all that behind you, Josie, soon enough."

"It's gone already," I said, tracing the pathway of a raindrop as it slid down the window.

It was true; it seemed to me that I had stopped being a little girl the day that Father died. Now I was stuck somewhere between being a child and a grown-up. Too young to make my own decisions, too old to hide away up here in the nursery.

"Come, Josie!" Before I could protest, Nanny Clay swept me up in a tight hug. "Things aren't so bleak as they seem. But you must watch your temper – especially when I'm gone."

"Gone?" I lifted my head and looked up into her old wrinkled face. "You ... you're not leaving, are you?" I stammered.

"I'm afraid so, pet." Her face was worried. "Her Ladyship downstairs gave me my marching orders the very first day she came."

"But ... Father promised you could stay at Summer's Place as long as you wanted to," I cried.

"He said we'd look after you one day, like you'd looked after us. Aunt Lavinia can't send you away. She can't!" First Merrylegs and now my dear old nanny. I thought my heart would break.

"Nothing was written down. It was a word of honour and there isn't a pinch of goodness left in this house. Not now." Nanny Clay nodded towards the door. "But don't you worry about me. My nephew lives in a pretty little village called Fairstowe. I'm sure he'll put up with me, provided I don't get under his feet."

"But . . . when do you go?"

"Tomorrow. After church." Nanny Clay stroked my hair.

Normally I would have pulled away, but today I clung to her, letting her hug me as we watched the rain against the window.

"A boiled egg and a jug of milk." She chuckled, straightening up at last. "Right over their heads? Now there's a thing I'd like to have seen."

And we both began to laugh.

I kept that memory with me the next day, as she turned and waved one last time at the churchyard gate.

She touched the silver locket around her neck. It

contained one lock of Father's hair and one of mine. Then she limped away, never looking back as she climbed into Farmer Sewell's dog cart, carrying all she'd ever owned in one small leather bag.

Chapter Five

Merrylegs snorted as my footsteps echoed on the stony stable floor. Every stall was empty now, except his.

So much had changed so quickly. Poor Nanny Clay was gone. So had all the horses, other than the pair to pull the carriage who were stabled in the coach house.

And first thing tomorrow morning Merrylegs would be gone too. "The coachman from Birtwick is coming to take you away along with a load of hay." I sniffed, laying my head against his dappled flank. "But you're not to worry." I straightened up and made my voice sound as clear and strong as I could. I am not daft enough to think that horses understand every word we say, but I do believe they know when we are scared or calm, happy or sad. I didn't want Merrylegs to leave knowing how desperate and hollow I felt inside.

"Birtwick Park will be a lovely home," I said brightly, "I heard old Thomas telling Billy all about it. It is a nice estate on the other side of the Beacon Hills. Squire Gordon keeps a fine stable," I explained, echoing Thomas's words before I added an extra reassurance of my own. "I am sure the children will be kind and gentle, and excellent riders who won't pull your mouth or jab you in the sides. You'll be spoiled rotten with apples and bran mash and hay..."

Merrylegs turned and nuzzled me, looking for a treat already.

I held out the lump of sugar I'd slipped inside my handkerchief at breakfast yesterday. Before I threw the egg at Aunt Lavinia's head. Before I knew this would be Merrylegs's last day.

"Greedy boy!" I scratched him between the ears. "Think what a fine adventure for you this will be..."

He nuzzled me again and I held back my tears ... right until the last moment when I kissed his soft grey nose and said goodbye.

As I hurried away through the empty stables,

Merrylegs scraped his hooves on the floor and whinnied for me to come back.

"I'm sorry, boy," I whispered. I did not want to let him see me crying. But it broke my heart to leave my little pony alone for the very last time.

It was dark outside. When I had dried my eyes, I crept into the house as quietly as a stable mouse.

But Aunt Lavinia was waiting.

"In here, Josephine," she called from the drawing room. "A word."

"Yes, Aunt," I said, digging my nails into my palm and trying to remember my promise to Nanny Clay. I would hold my temper. But I would not apologize. Never.

"After your horrid little tantrum, I have been reviewing your position here," said Aunt Lavinia. The sour-lime smile was back. "Your outburst yesterday morning was most troubling. Dear Eustace is so very sensitive. He cannot be exposed to such. . ."

"Violence," said Eustace.

"Exactly. In light of the unfortunate events at the breakfast table, I have written a letter." Aunt Lavinia waved a sheet of lilac notepaper. "I have asked Lady Hexham to take you on as her companion."

"Lady Hexham?"

"Please don't repeat what I say like a parrot." Aunt Lavinia sighed. "Honestly, Josephine, I shall have to ask Cook to find a piece of cuttlefish for you to chew on."

Eustace seemed to think this was hilarious. I ignored him.

"Who is Lady Hexham? I don't know anybody of that name," I said. "Why would she want me to be her companion?"

"Of course you don't know Lady Hexham!" Eustace snorted as if I had said something terrifically funny. "Nobody knows Lady Hexham. She is very old and never goes outside."

"She is a recluse," explained Aunt Lavinia. "She lives all alone in a big house. Nobody ever goes in and she never comes out."

It sounded terrible.

"That is why she needs a companion." Eustace snipped little his scissors in the air. "She gets bored all alone. It will be your job to amuse her."

"But I know nothing of old ladies," I protested. Surely this was some sort of joke. I couldn't be sent away to look after a dusty old lady all by myself.

"It seems you know very little of anything." Aunt

Lavinia sighed, pointing to the crumpled pile of table napkins I had been asked to embroider. "No needlepoint, no music, no singing. Nothing but horses and hay!"

"Does Lady Hexham have horses?" I asked, hopefully. "I would gladly ride with her, or..."

"Horses?" Aunt Lavinia and Eustace were laughing.

"What use would a housebound old lady have for horses?" snorted Aunt Lavinia. "The stables were closed up years ago. Honestly, Josephine. I knew you were wilful and spoiled. Now I see you are stupid as well. It is a good job you will be going away from this place. Consider it an opportunity for self-improvement. You can spend less time in a stable and more time perfecting the accomplishments of a young lady."

"B-but how long will it be for? Can I come home sometimes?" It wasn't Aunt Lavinia and Eustace who I would miss, of course. But I couldn't bear the thought of being parted from Summer's Place. Especially not now spring was here – the hedgerows would be full of wild flowers and blossom. The orchard and the churchyard too. The churchyard where Father lay. Who would visit his grave if I was gone?

"Hexham Hall is many miles away," said Aunt Lavinia. "You cannot expect to return here willynilly."

"Then when?" I asked.

"Not until the old lady dies," said Eustace with a horrid grin.

I felt a treacherous tear sting the corner of my eye but I would not let it fall.

"You must make yourself useful since your father left you so ill-provided for," said Aunt Lavinia. "Eustace is master now. You cannot expect to stay here and beg for charity. We might be family but we are not fools."

"Indeed," Eustace snorted. Their faces blurred. I had a horrid dizzy feeling. I have never fainted in my whole life. But the drawing room seemed to rock and sway like a pirate ship on the sea. I clutched the back of a chair. Everything I had ever known had been taken from me. First Father. Then Nanny Clay. Next Merrylegs. And now Summer's Place itself.

Somehow I managed to turn the door handle, escape into the hall, and flee.

Chapter Six

The nursery without Nanny Clay was as bleak as the empty stables.

Someone had lit the gas lamps. Perhaps a maid. But there was no mug of cocoa waiting. No one to help me out of my clothes or brush and plait my hair as Nanny Clay did every night. No one to scold me for saying my prayers too quickly.

I rang the bell five times but still nobody came. Aunt Lavinia must have told them not to. When I had struggled out of my dress, I sat in my petticoat sobbing on the end of my bed.

"Josephine Judith Green," I sniffed, staring at my red-eyed reflection. "This is ridiculous." I had never cried more than a dozen times in my whole life and now I seemed to cry a dozen times a day.

"Enough!" I said, standing up and turning to my mother's portrait. "I will put a brave face on. If they want to send me off to look after some horrid old spider who lives all alone, then I shall go. And I shall not let them see that I care." I nodded my head to the painting. "I shall be like you, Mother. I shall pretend I am an actress performing in a play." I held the edge of my petticoat and curtsyed.

I had never spoken out loud to Mother's picture before. I never needed to. Nanny Clay was always here. She certainly wouldn't have held with people chitter-chattering to portraits – especially not portraits of runaway mothers who had brought shame, not only on themselves, but the whole family.

"Well, she's not here to judge us now, is she, Mother?" I said. "I wish you were with me though. Perhaps if you had stayed, just a little longer, I might know more about needlepoint and music and singing. Things that might amuse a cross old lady. Aunt Lavinia is right: all I know about is horses."

I yanked off my petticoat and began to wriggle out of my bloomers. As I kicked my undergarments across the floor, I saw a neat pile of clothes on the window sill.

FOR THE VICARAGE — said a note in Nanny Clay's big round hand. Even on the day she was leaving, she had remembered to fold and press Billy's outgrown garments so that the parlour maid could take them to the village for the poor. Even his white long johns had been washed and dried.

"A stable lad's clothes," I said to myself, running my fingers over the coarse fabric of the ragged tweed waistcoat. "If only I could have a job with horses instead of old ladies. . ."

And then, with my hand still resting on the pile of old clothes, an astonishing idea came to me, an idea so exciting that my knees began to shake. What if I was to dress up as a boy? What if I was to take a job in a stable? Aunt Lavinia had said that working with horses was all I was fit for. And I knew there was a job going for a new stable lad at Birtwick Park – the very same place that Merrylegs was going in the morning. . .

If I disguised myself, I could hide in the load of hay and go with him.

When we reached Birtwick I could slip down from the cart and ask for the job. I could escape from Aunt Lavinia and The Slug. Merrylegs and I would never need to be separated after all.

It was a wild idea. Mad. But why not? My palms were sweating.

I took the long johns first, then grabbed the rough brown trousers from the bottom of the pile, sending everything else tumbling to the floor as I hopped on one foot, struggling to pull them on. Although Billy was broader and taller than I was now, these old outgrown clothes of his were baggy, but they weren't a bad fit. There was a long white shirt and a frayed belt, as well as a pair of short, scuffed boots. I stuffed a silk handkerchief in the toe of each and found the thick grey winter stockings Nanny Clay had knitted for me. If I tied the laces tight, the boots were snug enough. Lastly I grabbed Billy's flat cap and rolled my long red hair up into it.

"What do you think?" I asked Mother's picture. Although there was no one here to see me my heart was racing. All the dizziness from the drawing room was gone. It was excitement which made my head buzz now. But a glance in the looking glass wiped the smile from my face. The curls of hair escaping from the cap instantly betrayed me; it wouldn't fool anyone.

"People will see that I am a girl in an instant." I sighed, shaking my head as great red tresses tumbled down my back.

I pulled open the little drawer in the side of the dressing table. There was only one thing to be done. The nursery scissors glinted in the lamplight. With trembling hands I lifted them and began to cut.

It had taken a whole lifetime to grow my long red hair and in a matter of moments it was gone – a shaggy-haired urchin stared out at me from the looking glass.

Biting my lip, I examined my strange new reflection. I barely recognized the thin, speckled face which scowled back. Were my ears always so large? I peered more closely. My green eyes widened. Did I really have that many freckles on my nose? They seemed to stand out twice as much now the fringe of hair which framed my face was gone.

"I certainly don't look like you any longer, Mother," I said, glancing sadly at her portrait. If ever there had been any resemblance it was lost. While she was still a goddess, I looked like a startled hedgehog.

I swallowed hard. Thank goodness Nanny Clay wasn't here. It would break her heart. "Your crowning glory!" she always called my long red hair.

I scooped up the fallen curls from the floor, opened the window and flung them in to the orchard outside. Then, slipping off my boots but leaving my new clothes on, I curled up on top of the covers and tried to doze.

I left the window wide open so that the crowing cockerel in the chicken coop below would wake me at first light.

If I was going to be up in time to stow away with Merrylegs, I could not be late.

Chapter Seven

I was awake before the cockerel crowed.

I leapt up and stuffed my feet inside Billy's well-worn boots. In the half-light, I gasped in surprise as I caught sight of my short hair in the looking glass. But there was no going back.

I turned to Mother's portrait for the last time.

"I wonder if you came and said goodbye to me when you ran away," I whispered. She had left a note for Father. But nothing at all for me.

I had found the sheet of pretty blue paper tucked into a cedar box on Father's desk one rainy day and read it secretly. But when I went back a few days later, the note was gone and I glimpsed a scrap of burnt blue paper in the grate.

It was not a long letter. I still remember every word it said.

Dear Charles,
  I am going back to London. I am suited neither for motherhood nor for country life. Do not look for me.
  Your dearest,
  Valentina.

Father took her at her word. He did not try to find her.

"If she wants to come back, she knows we are here," he always said. "I do not wish to hunt her like a fox."

She never did come back.

I reached up to touch her pale hand in the portrait. "Goodbye, Mother. I hope you are happy wherever you ran to," I whispered, pulling Billy's cap firmly down on my head. "It's my turn for adventure now..."

Then I ran – out of the nursery door and down the stairs without ever looking back.

*

I was amazed by the noise my footsteps made in

Billy's heavy boots. The leather on my own riding boots was as thin and smooth as a linen bed sheet. These clodhoppers were as thick and wrinkled as the hide of a rhinoceros. I had to tiptoe all the way to the stables. As I turned the corner I was surprised to see old Thomas already in the yard with a broom in his hand.

I ducked back behind the tack shed wall.

The cobbles were as clean as a dinner plate but Thomas still seemed to find something to sweep up.

"I shall miss this," he said, calling over his shoulder to Merrylegs. "But I'm too old for anyone new to take me on." He paused and leant against his broom for a moment, wheezing.

I felt a pang of guilt. I had never stopped to think that with the horses gone there would be no more work for Thomas either. He had been at Summer's Place since my grandfather's day.

"Well, Merrylegs, lad," he said, giving himself a little shake. "You've got a fine day for it."

He was right. The pink glow of the morning sunrise was still hanging in the air, but golden-yellow rays were creeping in now too.

As Thomas began to sweep again, I heard the

plodding slap of hooves and a big roan cob pulling an empty hay cart clattered down the lane.

This is it, I thought. The man from Birtwick Park had arrived.

Thomas stepped forward and shook hands with the driver.

"John Manly, coachman to Squire Gordon," said the big sandy-haired man, lifting his cap as he jumped down from the seat. He was middle-aged. Perhaps a little younger than Father, but tall with broad shoulders like a bear.

The very first thing he did was to loosen the harness on the roan cob.

"We'll let old Justice breathe a bit before we turn around." He grinned.

"Good idea," said Thomas, fetching a small scoop of oats and a shallow pail of water for the horse. Then the two grooms took pitchforks and began to fill the cart with hay.

"Strange to think they'll not need fodder here next winter. It's a sad day that sees the end of the famous Summer's Place stud," said Mr Manly.

"Aye. As soon as you take the little pony, I'll be off myself," said Thomas. "I don't suppose I'll ever be back. Except perhaps to visit the churchyard and pay my respects to the master."

"Thank you!" I whispered under my breath, grateful to think that Father would never be quite alone.

Then, when a fat mound of hay was piled on the cart, the two grooms turned towards Merrylegs's stall at last.

"Let's fetch the little fellow. He's a fine pony," said Thomas.

With a pounding heart, I took my chance, shot out from behind the tack shed and dived into the cart, burying myself beneath the mountain of hay.

I had only been hidden for a moment when I heard Thomas tying Merrylegs to the back of the cart with a rope.

"You be good, little fellow," he whispered. "You might not be the biggest or grandest chap we ever had at Summer's Place, but I'll miss you all the same."

Then there was a creak of wood above my head as Mr Manly heaved himself up on the seat.

I held my breath, terrified that I would sneeze as the hay tickled my nose.

"Ready, Justice?" The coachman clicked his tongue and the cart moved at last.

I had done it. We were off. I was escaping from Aunt Lavinia and The Slug. I wriggled a little, pulling Billy's cap over my nose and mouth to keep the dusty hay from my face.

"Stop! Wait!" The cart pulled up sharply as I heard old Thomas shout.

I froze. Had he seen me move?

His footsteps ran along beside of the cart. "Don't forget your pitchfork, Mr Manly."

"Thank you." The wooden bench squeaked as the coachman turned around. "Just toss it in the back, will you?"

I smiled with relief. They hadn't seen me after all.

There was a heavy thud.

"Ouch!" The sharp prong of the pitchfork jabbed me behind the knee. Only the thick blanket of hay stopped me from being stabbed right through.

"Did you hear that?" I froze as Thomas's voice sounded above my head. He was leaning right down over the cart.

"Hear what?" said Mr Manly.

"A squeak," said Thomas.

I was sure they would hear my thundering heart.

"Must be a rat," said Mr Manly. "It'll soon jump out once we're on our way."

"Reckon you're right," said Thomas with a dry laugh. "Even the rats don't want to stay at

Summer's Place now."

Then the grooms called goodbye to each other, the cart shuddered and we were off again.

The only sound now was the flat clop-clop of the cob's big feet and the jolly clip-clip of Merrylegs tied behind. But it was a long time until I dared to move.

We must have been rattling along the lane for ten minutes before I wriggled to the back of the cart. I peered through the hay, hoping I could still see Summer's Place. I would have loved one last view of the big white house and the stable clock. But we were trotting along between tall hedges and all I could see was the church spire. As the bright morning sun caught the weathervane on the top, I thought of Father lying in his grave below. It was as if he was sending me his blessing.

"Goodbye," I whispered. "God rest your soul."

Then Merrylegs saw me peeping out of the hay and whinnied in delight.

"Shh!" I warned him putting my fingers to my lips. "You mustn't give me away."

The cart rocked as we turned another corner and when I looked up again the steeple was lost in the distance. My old life at Summer's Place had slipped away.

Part Two

Birtwick Park

Chapter Eight

Justice the old cob plodded on along the lanes. The day was hot and I was soon sweltering beneath the hay. With the rocking of the cart, I began to feel drowsy. After my restless night and early start, I must have dropped off.

The next thing I knew, the air was cooler and I was woken with a start.

The cart had stopped.

"Steady, lads," said Mr Manly in a soothing way. From under the hay, I could see that Merrylegs's ears were pricked and the cart shook as calm old Justice fussed and fretted in the shafts.

What was going on?

I heard the thud of galloping hooves in the

distance. Merrylegs and the old cob both whinnied. They were answered with an excited neigh from far away across the fields. I could hear raised voices shouting in the distance too.

The cart creaked as Mr Manly shifted.

"Come on, Justice. Sounds like there's trouble at Birtwick," he said clicking his tongue. "Trot on. We best get home. . ."

Birtwick? So we were nearly there.

Justice had broken into a brisk trot.

The raised voices were still shouting far off. There seemed to be quite some hullabaloo – as if a large crowd had gathered. I could hear frantic neighs too. Urged on by the coachman, Justice had begun to canter. On the end of his rope, little Merrylegs was lolloping along behind. There wasn't a moment to lose if I wanted to get out of the hay unseen.

"See you later, Merry . . . at Birtwick Park!" I whispered as I wriggled to the back of the cart. I was going to have to jump. I tried not to look down at the ground whizzing past. If this went wrong, I would break my back on the rough stones or Merrylegs would trample me with his hooves before he could even try and stop.

With shaky hands, I pulled Billy's cap tight down

on my head, closed my eyes and leapt sideways, praying I would land on the soft grass at the edge of the lane.

Whump! The wind was knocked out of me … but the ground was soft and mossy. I had landed on the verge. I opened one eye and rolled towards the high hedge, staying low in case Mr Manly turned his head. Thank goodness for Billy's loose-fitting clothes. I would never have managed this in my skirts and petticoat. Not even in my riding habit.

As my breath returned, I lay back and smiled. I had done it. I had run away from home. I had leapt from a speeding cart. I was free.

As soon as the cart disappeared around the corner, I scrambled on to all fours. The bushes were flecked with wool and there was a small round hole in the bottom of the hedge which looked as if it might have been made by a sheep. I pushed my way through, eager to be off the public lane so I could sit a moment, steady myself and think.

But, as soon as I came out into the field on the other side, I blinked and gasped with surprise.

A beautiful black horse was galloping towards me. His saddle was hanging upside down beneath his belly, the stirrups flying up against his flanks. His reins were in a tangle too. His eyes were wild. But in spite of his disarray, he was the most incredible horse I had ever seen.

As I raised my head, I saw that the group of men I had heard were shouting and waving their arms from the next field as they sprinted in this direction. I could see the long, low shape of a stable block behind them.

Birtwick, I presumed. The horse must have bolted from home.

As he reached the hedge I had scrambled through he began to spin in wild circles, his long black tail held high with nerves. I saw the reins were caught around his leg; he might fall and break his neck.

"Whoa! Steady, boy." I stepped forward and held out my hand towards him.

The horse skidded to a halt and stared at me, his ears pricked, ready to turn and bolt at any moment. At least he had stopped galloping. But his flanks were heaving and he snorted like a dragon.

I took another step forward and he threw his head in the air, rearing up in panic as the rein pulled against his leg.

"Shh. Don't be afraid." He had got himself in a terrible frenzy. If only I still had one of Merrylegs's sugar lumps to offer him, then perhaps I could reach out and take hold of his bridle.

I looked down and saw that the front of Billy's rough tweed waistcoat was covered with hay from the cart.

"Here, boy. It is not quite a sugar lump … but it is fresh and sweet." I gathered the loose strands into a bunch and held the hay towards him as if I was a gentleman offering a lady a bouquet of flowers.

The frightened horse stretched out his nose and sniffed. He was big and beautiful – shiny black all over except for one white sock on his front leg and a perfect white star right in the middle of his forehead. The most beautiful creature I had ever set eyes on.

"You must be hungry after all that galloping," I urged as he sniffed the hay again.

I noticed that the men had stopped shouting. Even from so far away they must have realized I was having some success and were holding back to see what happened next.

The horse nibbled the top of my bouquet of hay. I held my breath as I leant forward and slipped my fingers under the noseband of his bridle.

"Got you!" I said gently. I did not want to tug on the reins while they were still around his leg. But as he pulled the hay from my fingers and began to chew it, I raised my other arm and scratched between his ears. He let out a low sigh and lowered his velvet nose into my hand.

"There. Just like Merrylegs." I laughed. "A big softy after all."

The young horse watched me, still breathing heavily. He was even more wonderful close up than he had been from far away. His dark intelligent eyes blinked as he flared his nostrils.

"I wonder what your name is?" I whispered, letting him get used to the sound of my voice. "Maybe Ebony? Or Midnight? Just plain old Blackie, perhaps?" No. None of these seemed quite right. It would have to be something grand and beautiful. I had never seen a horse like him.

Still whispering, I ran my hand down his leg. He seemed to trust me at last and obediently lifted his hoof as I unlooped the tangled rein.

"There, that's better isn't it?" I said, holding the loose reins like a rope. I kept one hand close to the bit in his mouth. But, as soon as I tried to lead him forward, I realized we would have to do something about the saddle too. It was still hanging upside down underneath his belly.

I took one hand from the reins and patted his neck, moving gently towards his back. I had to stretch up to reach. He was so much bigger than Merrylegs. Fifteen or nearly sixteen hands perhaps. He was only a little smaller than Father's hunter, Magnum, but of a much lighter build.

I patted his back and sides all around the upside-down saddle, stroking and soothing him. He turned his head to watch but didn't shy away.

At last, I was brave enough to give a tug, but the saddle wouldn't shift. I would have to try and unfasten it instead. As I pulled aside the leather flap I saw what had made the saddle slip in the first place. The strap holding the girth was almost frayed right through and hanging by just a few strong threads. I fumbled with the buckle.

Thump! The saddle hit the ground. The big black horse sprung forward again in fright. But I still had hold of the reins.

"Steady," I coaxed, stretching out my hand until he let me rub his nose again. "You're not a fighter, I can see that. You've had a fright. But look – now that silly old saddle is gone."

I glanced across the big field towards the stable block where the men were watching.

"Well done, lad," called one of them and I smiled to myself. I had almost forgotten I looked like a boy.

"Come on then," I said, leaving the saddle lying in the mud and walking the magnificent horse beside me. "Time to take you back home."

Everyone had said Squire Gordon had a fine stable at Birtwick Park. But I had never dreamed of a horse as magnificent as this.

Chapter Nine

I was heading down the field, leading the big horse as placidly as a lamb when I saw Mr Manly waving his arms. He had joined the group of men on the other side of a long stone wall which ran between us.

"Well done there, young fellow!" he called out, breathing hard from running. He had no idea who I was, of course, or that just ten minutes ago I had been hiding beneath his load of hay. "It is a great service you have done us," he hollered over the wall. I gave him what I hoped was a boyish grin, not daring to speak.

"Quite so," boomed a well-spoken man in pale riding breeches who I assumed must be Squire Gordon himself. "But I am afraid there is no gate down here, lad. You cannot get him home this way." He pointed to the high stone wall between us. The horse must have jumped it when he bolted. It was sharp and jagged. I glanced at his legs and ran my hand softly along his belly. He was lucky not to have cut himself to shreds on the way over.

"It would be best if you could bring him round by the lane. There is a gate just beyond that little wood in the far corner of the field." Mr Manly raised his arm, pointing towards a group of trees behind me.

"We'd be most obliged if you could bring him home that way, young chap," added the squire.

I grinned like a jack-o'-lantern. They had called me *lad* and *fellow* and now *young chap*. They were convinced I was a boy! If I could just bring the squire's horse home safely, surely I could at least ask about the stable job...

"Right away," I answered, surprised how loud and deep my voice sounded as I tried my best to holler like a farmer's son.

"He's a big horse, but he won't hurt you," called Mr Manly. "Don't worry about Black Beauty. He's as good as gold."

"Black Beauty!" I smiled, stroking the white star

in the middle of the horse's forehead. "Of course that is your name. It is perfect."

I turned his head, ready to walk back across the field. I was afraid he might dig his hooves in as I tried to lead him in the opposite direction to home. But he seemed to trust me. I clicked my tongue and he followed without even a tug on the reins.

"Thank you, Black Beauty," I whispered, glowing inside. "Let's get you back to Birtwick. We're going to be the very best of friends, I am sure."

We walked calmly back across the field and slipped behind the wood, out of sight of the stables.

"Stupid knot!" I must have tugged at the thick rope tied around the gate for at least ten minutes. Still it would not budge. Whoever had tied it had pulled the knot so tight there was no way to get my fingers inside and wiggle it free.

"If only I had a knife," I groaned, searching the ground for a sharp stone.

Black Beauty jostled me with his nose. It was as though he was trying to tell me something.

"That's not going to help." I laughed, but inside I started to panic. Mr Manly and the squire would wonder what was taking me so long. They would think I had stolen the beautiful horse if I didn't return to the stables soon. I'd wanted so much to be quick, to prove to them that I was reliable – the perfect boy to be a stable lad. Now they'd scold me for dilly-dallying and send me off with a clip around the ear.

Perhaps if I really was a boy, I would know all about knots. I remember Father telling me once that sailors have at least a hundred different ways to tie a rope at sea. All I knew was how to unpick tangled embroidery ... and that was only because I went wrong so much.

"Stupid thing!" I kicked the gate and cursed as loud as any sailor. With the gate tied tight, our path was blocked.

"There's no point fussing." I sighed. "Our way is barred and that's all there is to it. What else can we do?"

I turned and stared helplessly across the landscape.

As Beauty shook his head and fidgeted, I had a sudden thought. He couldn't jump over the gate – especially not on to the hard lane beyond – but where the field rolled away to the left of us, I saw there was a broad ditch at the bottom running along beside the soft ground of the meadow beyond. If we could just get across that, it would lead us straight up to the stables from the other side. Any horse as strong as Beauty could jump it easily.

"What do you think? Will you let me ride you?" I looked up into his eyes and Beauty stopped fidgeting right away and stared back at me. Perhaps it was because my voice was serious all of a sudden, but he seemed almost to sense how desperately I needed his help. I felt a connection between us in that moment – as if we had made a bond.

"All right," I said. "We'll do it!"

If I stopped to think about my plan I would lose my nerve. I climbed on to a fallen tree at the edge of the wood and scrambled on to his back from there. The minute he felt my weight, Beauty skittered and swished his tail. He probably wasn't used to being ridden bareback and I certainly wasn't used to riding like this either.

"Ready?" I said, gathering up a bunch of his soft jet-black mane along with the reins. "Let's get you home."

With one tiny squeeze of my legs he was off – shooting forward so quickly I almost fell right back over his tail. But I clung on tight, gripping his bare flanks with my knees.

As we cantered away across the field, I wanted to shout for joy. If riding stout little Merrylegs felt like being on a rocking horse, clinging to Black Beauty was like flying through the sky on Pegasus. The ground flattened out, and my heart soared as he broke into a gallop, his hooves barely seeming to touch the earth at all.

Thank goodness I had practised riding like a boy. But never before had I ridden bareback. There was a small tight knot of fear right in the pit of my stomach but, more than that, I felt fluttery with exhilaration. My fingertips – and even my toes deep inside the heavy borrowed boots – seemed to fizz with excitement.

The men were shouting as we galloped into view of the stables again. I wasn't sure if they were yelling for me stop, turn back or carry on. But I paid no attention, blocking out their voices like the cawing of crows.

I had made my choice to bring Black Beauty home this way. It was too late to change my mind. I had to get us both there safely. All my concentration was focused on just one thing. We had to leap the huge ditch at the bottom of the meadow.

Chapter Ten

I clung to Beauty's neck. The closer we galloped the wider the ditch began to look. I swallowed hard. It was as broad as the dining table at Summer's Place.

By now, Aunt Lavinia would know I was gone. Never again would I have to sit across that same table, watching Cousin Eustace slurp runny yolk from his soft boiled eggs. The thought of that made me feel braver at once. Here I was about to leap bareback over a chasm, but I would rather jump a pit of snakes than face another dreary meal with Aunt Lavinia and The Slug.

"Steady now," I warned Black Beauty. We needed speed to clear the ditch but mustn't rush it.

At the very last moment I let him have his head,

holding more of his mane than the reins. "Go on, Black Beauty, I trust you!" I whispered.

His ears pricked. It was as though he understood.

Up, up, up we flew.

Time seemed to freeze as if someone had held the hands of a clock. I let out a whoop of excitement as the wind whistled past my ears. The sound surprised me. It was a noise I had never made before. A sort of wild cry.

Then thud. We landed safely on the other side. I hit my chin hard against his neck. But Black Beauty was brilliant. He barely broke his stride as we galloped on.

A great roar went up from the men. Perhaps it was a cheer or perhaps a gasp of shock. I wasn't sure.

"Steady, Beauty." I pulled on the reins. Now we were clear of the ditch I slowed him to a canter and then to a gentle trot. By the time we were close enough to see the faces of the men, I had calmed him right down to a walk. But my stomach was squirming with a fear far worse than galloping bareback or leaping a giant ditch. I was about to have to prove myself – as a boy.

*

Ten minutes later, I was beneath a magnificent stable clock, stammering out my request to Squire Gordon.

It was half past four in the afternoon. Back home, Aunt Lavinia would have rung for tea in the stuffy drawing room, pulling the curtains closed to spare Eustace from the light.

Squire Gordon tugged at his dark moustache as he stared down at me in surprise. "What's this you say? You want a job, lad? Here? Working with the horses?"

"Yes, sir," I mumbled, half in fear and half to keep my voice low and gruff like a farmhand. "I – I heard there was an opening."

I was standing in front of the squire and Mr Manly in the airy, red-brick stable yard. The other men – gardeners and shepherds – had wandered back to their work while a dark, moody-looking stable boy scowled at me and led Black Beauty away. I had no idea why he should look so angry... Perhaps he disapproved of the jump I had made.

I explained at once how I had been unable to loosen the knot on the top gate and had decided it best to ride Black Beauty home. There had been so much fuss and chatter, so many questions as everybody clustered around Beauty, checking him for wounds and scrapes, that I wasn't sure yet if I was to be scolded for foolishness or praised for being brave.

My legs were still shaking from the great leap over the ditch and it did now seem a reckless, daredevil thing to have done.

"You certainly took matters into your own hands," said the squire with a sigh. "I do not know if that makes you irresponsible or quick thinking."

I lifted my head, making sure to look politely at the squire, but said nothing, just as I had seen the youngest servants do many times when Father spoke to them at home.

"You brought Black Beauty safely back to us. And for that we are grateful," he said. Then he spoke to his coachman. "What do you think, Manly? We do need a new stable lad but it is up to you to choose whom we employ. The stables are your domain. You are master here."

Mr Manly said nothing for a moment, but towered over me like a great bear. I might have turned and fled if it wasn't for the fact that his eyes were kind and full of light.

"Hmm," he said at last. "Tell me, young fellow, have you worked in a stable before?"

"I – I have been around horses all my life," I said. That at least was true.

He nodded, as if pleased with the answer. "And your folks?"

It took me a moment to realize he was asking about my parents.

"I – I'm an orphan," I said. With Father dead and a runaway mother who had left me so long ago, I might as well have been.

"And where is it that you have come from?" asked the squire.

"From Summer's Place." Again, I decided truth – or at least a slice of it – might be best. If questioned, I could describe our estate better than any other. "It's beyond the Beacon hills, sir. The stables have been all closed up since the old master was ... since he was killed." The words caught in my throat but the squire put his hand on my shoulder.

"Terrible business. Terrible. . ."

"I have come from there just now," said Mr Manly. "If I had known you were heading this way I could have given you a lift on the hay cart."

"Oh ... how kind." I felt my cheeks flush scarlet.

"I was collecting this little chappy for the young ladies. Maybe he is a friend of yours?" said Mr

Manly, leading me into a stable with three stalls where horses could be tied up and a big loose box where another could stand free. Merrylegs raised his head from the first stall and whinnied with excitement.

I longed to rush forward and throw my arms around his neck. But I just nodded quickly.

I noticed the tall, dark-haired stable boy still scowling at me through the bars of the loose box where he tended to Black Beauty. What had I done to make him look so furious?

Forcing myself to hold back, I stretched out my hand and rubbed Merrylegs's nose as he nuzzled against me.

"I'm sure the children here will be very happy with him. Merrylegs is a wonderful pony," I said.

"And he's pleased to see you," Mr Manly said with a smile. "That's better than any reference written down on paper. If you were cruel or lazy or wicked, he would shy away and lay his ears down flat against his head."

Good old Merrylegs!

"So what do you think, Manly?" said the squire. "Shall we give this young lad a chance? He's a fine horseman. We've seen that from the way he rode."

Mr Manly nodded. "I have never seen Beauty so well matched," he said in his deep gentle voice. "It was as if you and the young horse were made for each other, lad. Quite extraordinary."

Pride was bubbling up inside me like a spring. They thought I was well-matched with the magnificent Black Beauty.

"You're the bravest young chap I've ever seen," agreed the squire, clapping me on the back. "You wouldn't catch me leaping a ditch like that without a saddle..."

"Really?" I did a little dance of joy. I couldn't help myself. A good horseman? Me?

The squire laughed but Mr Manly cleared his throat.

"I can't give you the job until I know one more thing," he said.

I stopped jiggling and my heart froze in my chest.

"What is it?" Would it be something I could answer? Or something only a real stable lad would know?

"Well," said Mr Manly, taking a step closer. "We do not even know your name..."

"Oh! Is that all..." My heart started thudding again and I smiled as the coachman held out his huge hand for me to shake. I could not be Josephine any more of course – or Josie. But I had planned for this, remembering how Farmer Sewell always pretended to greet young Master Joseph when I rode past his farm like a boy.

"My name is Joseph Green," I said. "But ... but they call me Joe."

Joe Green. I liked the sound of that.

"Welcome to Birtwick Park, young Joe," said Mr Manly. "The job is yours, provided you do it well."

"Thank you! I won't let you down," I said. "I promise." But I had to steady myself against the side of the stall for a moment.

I had done it. My new life – *Joe Green's* new life – was about to begin.

Chapter Eleven

Squire Gordon and Mr Manly strolled to Black Beauty's loose box and peered over the door. I followed, almost skipping; I was so happy about my new job. Then I remembered to take big, heavy steps and stride like a country boy.

Black Beauty turned his head and stared at us with his eyes bright and his ears pricked. He was none the worse for our adventure and seemed to be enjoying the careful grooming the stable boy was giving him.

"How did he come to bolt in the first place?" I asked.

The stable lad shot me a look as sharp as a dagger.

"The saddle slipped while he was galloping. Gave

him quite a fright, so I hear," said Mr Manly.

"Nobody's fault. Could have happened to anyone," said the squire.

But as the stable boy bent his dark head to brush Black Beauty's hock I saw his breeches were covered with fresh wet mud.

So *he* had been the one riding Beauty . . . it looked like he had taken quite a tumble. But there was no need to glare at me as though it was my fault. I had saved his skin by bringing the horse home safely.

At least he seemed to bear Beauty no ill will. He patted him and stepped out of the loose box.

"Listen up, Joe," said Mr Manly. "This here is James Howard, our senior stable lad. Whatever he tells you to do, you do it. He will be in charge of you from now on."

"Pleased to meet you, James." I held out my hand but the boy just grunted. I guessed he was only a year or two older than me but my head barely reached his shoulder.

"We've decided to give young Joe a chance," said Squire Gordon. "It seemed only fair after he saved the day just now. And he rode Black Beauty home with such great skill."

"Yes, sir," agreed James, nodding to his master. I

saw a muscle twitch in the side of his cheek as he stared at his boots.

That's what it is, I thought. *He's jealous.*

"We'll leave you to it," said Mr Manly, heading off with the squire across the yard. "James will show you the ropes, Joe. You're in good hands."

"Thank you, Mr Manly. Thank you for the opportunity," I said.

But, as I turned to face James again, he narrowed his flashing grey eyes and frowned.

"I don't think it was great skill you showed, bringing the horse home like that, Joe Green. It was nothing but showing off and circus tricks," he said.

"But—" I felt as if I had been slapped in the face. "I rode Black Beauty back safely. Isn't that all that matters?" I asked.

"You were lucky. You took a gamble and it paid off," said James. "But your silly stunt put the horse in danger."

I blushed furiously and bit my lip. If he knew who I really was, he would never dare to scold me like that.

But what he said next sent me reeling.

"There was a master of a big house killed just a few weeks ago. Took a foolish leap in the hunting field. Too big for him. Too big for his horse."

He was talking about Father. . .

"Luckily, the horse survived," said James quietly. "But the idiot riding him died."

"Idiot?" I felt my knees buckle. "How dare you say that? You didn't even know him."

"Don't need to." James shrugged. "I know his type. Gets himself a big new thoroughbred. Wants to show it off to the other gentry. . . All for the sake of killing a fox."

"It wasn't like that," I spluttered. "Not really. . ."

"You knew him?" James looked surprised.

"Yes! I knew him. He was my. . ." I stopped barely able to swallow, let alone speak. "He was my . . . my master. Up at Summer's Place."

"I'm sorry." James's dark cheeks reddened. "I didn't know."

"Well, you do now," I said, hearing my voice go high like a girl. But I didn't care. "He was a fine horseman. At least he didn't go around falling off all the time just because his saddle slipped."

I had been going to tell James about the frayed strap, so he would know it really wasn't his fault. But I wouldn't bother. Not now.

"That reminds me," he said. "You had no business

leaving the saddle up there in the field. It's French. Worth more than you'll earn in a year. Five years on the pittance you'll be paid. You should have brought it back with you."

"How on earth was I supposed to do that?" I snapped. "I was riding bareback!"

"Exactly," snorted James as if that proved a point. "Walk up there now and fetch it. When you come back, I hope you'll have had time to cool off and improve your attitude, Joe Green. I don't know what passed for manners at Summer's Place but I am head stable boy at Birtwick Park and you'll do as I say without fuss."

The French saddle weighed a ton. I was still fuming as I staggered home with it. The stirrups clanged against my knees and I couldn't even see my feet as I tripped back down the lane.

It was six o'clock by the stable clock when I finally reached the yard. My arms ached from carrying the saddle. My legs burned from clinging tight to Beauty. My head felt light and my stomach churned with hunger. I hadn't had a crumb to eat since lunchtime the day before.

Two boys in garden smocks were dipping hunks

of bread into deep white bowls as they stretched out in the sun against the low wall.

"Suppertime," I gasped. "Thank goodness."

"Not for you." The first boy laughed. As they looked up I saw they both had shaggy blonde hair, big ears and sticky-out teeth. I couldn't tell one from the other.

"You won't get supper till you've dealt with that lot." The second boy nodded his head towards the stables. "The horses will need oats and hay before you get your broth."

He dipped his bread again.

"That's the good thing about spuds and cauliflowers. They don't kick and holler if you ignore 'em for a while," added the first boy, glancing over his shoulder towards the kitchen garden. "I'm Wilf, by the way, and this is Sid," he said, talking with his mouth full as he hungrily dipped his bread again.

"We're twins, in case you hadn't spotted." Sid laughed. "We work in the garden."

"I'm Joe," I said, without even a blink. I was getting used to the sound of my new name. "Stable lad."

"And circus rider, so we've heard," said Wilf with a whistle. "Quite a commotion you caused."

Oh no. I didn't want to start all that again.

Especially as I saw James coming across the yard towards us.

"I'd better get this put away," I said, heaving the saddle into my arms again and trying not to groan. The heaviest thing I had ever carried up until now was my thick leather-bound book on the kings and queens of England. My old governess, Miss Witchell, was forever testing me on great long passages I was supposed to learn by heart.

"Best get those horses fed," said one of the twins. I think it was Wilf but they had stood up and moved so I had no way of telling which was which. "James looks like he's in a fit of fury."

James was stomping back and forward across the yard with pitchforks of hay.

"Everything's got late, on account of all that kerfuffle," said Sid (or perhaps Wilf).

"Right." I knew I ought to go, but watched hungrily as the twins tossed the end of their bread to the pretty white birds who flew down from the dovecote. My stomach rumbled as I staggered away with the saddle.

"See you tonight, Joe," they called.

"Tonight?" I looked back over my shoulder.

"You'll be sleeping in the loft with the rest of us

lads." The twin pointed to a row of narrow windows below the stable clock.

Bedtime? I hadn't even thought about where a stable lad like me would sleep. But, of course, it would be with the other outdoor servant boys.

Where would I wash? What if I needed the lavatory? I had sneaked into the wood at the top field when I went to fetch the saddle . . . but I couldn't do that every time.

Being a boy – a stable boy – was going to be much harder than I thought. . .

Chapter Twelve

The bread was thick and dry. I think the soup was potato, but it could have been turnip. I wasn't sure. It was lumpy and cold by the time I came to eat it, sitting on the ground with my back against the wall as Wilf and Sid had done. By then, the sun was sinking and I had swept the yard and carried hay and water to each of the eighteen horses stabled there. I was so hungry I really think I would have stuck my head in Merrylegs's manger and shared his oats if that was all there was.

Half an hour later, I fell exhausted on to the thin straw-stuffed mattress in the loft above the stables. The floorboards and rafters were bare and strips of sacking covered the window to keep out the draughts. But I could have been sinking into my own feather bed, the mattress felt so soft and welcoming.

The other boys wore their long johns and shirts to sleep in, so I did the same. There was no talk of washing and to my relief there was a tumbledown privy at the edge of the kitchen garden. It was dark and full of spiders' webs and I had to perch with my bare bottom over a hole in a wooden board. But at least the little stone shed had a rickety door I could close to be alone and go to the lavatory like a girl.

All I wanted now was to shut my eyes and sleep.

"So Joe, tell us your story," said one of the twins eagerly, as I laid my head on my lumpy pillow. "Tell us how you came to Birtwick Park."

"Tomorrow," I murmured, rolling over to face the rough whitewashed wall. Despite dozing all the way here in the hay cart, I had never been so exhausted in my whole life. After all, I'd had to be up before dawn to run away from Summer's Place this morning.

"Goodnight." I pulled the bristly blanket up around my shoulders and snuggled down for a long deep sleep.

*

"Joe! Joe Green! Get up."

Someone was shouting.

"Who do you think you are? Queen Victoria in Windsor Castle? There's horses to be fed."

It seemed I had only been asleep for a moment, but as I sat up and rubbed my eyes, I saw the top of James's dark head disappearing down the ladder from the loft.

"Hurry up!" he barked.

I crawled forward and lifted the sacking curtains on the narrow window above my bed. It was barely light outside. Surely we didn't need to be up so soon?

I glanced around the loft, squinting in the grey light.

Will and Sid's mattresses were empty too, their blankets left in a tangled mess. But James's covers were pulled up neat and flat as if they had been smoothed with an iron.

"I'll be with you ... in just one minute," I said, flopping back on to my bed and closing my eyes. It was only for a moment.

Splash! Something cold and wet hit me in the face.

"Help! What's that?" I leapt to my feet and blinked.

81

An enormous, thick-set boy with small piggy eyes was standing over my bed. He had an empty metal pail in his hand and I was dripping from head to toe.

"You . . . you threw a bucket of water over me," I gasped.

"Reckon I did." The big youth snorted. "Is that why you screamed like a girl?"

"I didn't!" I said, grabbing the blanket and trying to mop myself down. But I could hear that my voice was still high-pitched and screechy. Worse, my hands were shaking.

"Who are you anyway?" I said, trying to growl from deep in my chest. "I was fast asleep, you know."

"Exactly!" The boy scratched his armpit. "I'm Caleb Trotter, carthorse groom. He pointed out of the window towards the back of the stable block where the working cobs and plough horses were kept. "His Majesty James the First said you needed waking."

"James the First?" What was he talking about.

"King James, as I calls him." Caleb snorted like a hog again, showing off a row of chipped yellow teeth. "I'm two years older than His Majesty. Yet he thinks he's so high and mighty, just cos he's looking after the fancy riding horses and I've got the heavy brutes instead."

"James Howard, the stable boy?" I asked. "He told you to pour a bucket of water over me?" I grabbed my trousers, hopping on one foot as I pulled them up over my soaking long johns. "Well, we'll see about that!" I grabbed my waistcoat from the wooden crate which served as both a table and a chair beside my bed. James wouldn't get away with this. I would report him to Squire Gordon if I had to . . . I was sure the squire knew my father.

Then I remembered that I didn't have a father. Not any more. And I don't suppose the squire cared what went on amongst his stable boys so long as his tack was polished and his horses were kept fit.

"James didn't actually tell me to throw the bucket of water." said Caleb, laughing. "He just said to come and check you was up. Soaking you was my own idea!"

"Horrid brute!" I lunged at him. But the only person I'd ever had a fist fight with was Cousin Eustace when I was five years old. It turned out Caleb was a whole lot stronger than that.

"Quite the little weasel, aren't you," he hissed,

grabbing my head under his arm and twisting my neck like a corkscrew.

"Ouch!" I stamped on his toes. But it was hopeless – I was still in my stocking feet. He had his huge heavy work boots on.

He picked me up under one arm as if I was no more than a bundle of hay and bumped me down the ladder from the loft.

"Hey, King James," he called, throwing me over his shoulder now like a sack of oats. "I got your stinking boy for you. Reckon he needs to cool down!"

I was still kicking and squirming and fighting but it did no good.

Caleb heaved me off his shoulder and dumped me – splosh – right in the middle of the horses' water trough.

"Ah!" It was freezing cold.

James stood with his hands on his hips looking furious. But he said nothing. It was hard to tell if he was cross with me or Caleb or both of us. The twins had come to see what the commotion was too.

"At least you're nice and clean now, Joe," said one of them. I think it was Sid – he had bigger ears.

"Saves you having a bath," agreed Wilf, giggling.

That did it. I stood up in the trough and shook my dripping fists at them all, swearing like I'd once heard Billy do when a tearaway colt of Father's kicked him in the knee.

"Control yourself, or you'll have Mr Manly to answer to," barked James.

"Fiery temper that one!" sneered Caleb. "It's the red hair that does it!"

"Just like Ginger." Sid sounded amused.

"Who's Ginger?" Another stable boy who'd want to challenge me as well? "Bring him out here and I'll fight him right now," I roared.

"Steady on. Ginger's a girl," Wilf said, grinning.

"A girl?" I lowered my fists. I must have looked like an idiot, standing dripping wet in the water trough.

"Ginger is a horse." Caleb sniggered. "You'll meet her soon enough."

Chapter Thirteen

I stood, wet as a drowned rat, in front of James, while Caleb sloped back off to the carthorses.

"Go to the laundry," James said with a sigh. "Have them dry those soggy clothes and find you something else to wear meanwhile."

Now all the fight was gone from me, I felt close to tears. I turned my back and walked away without a word.

"Wait, Joe!" James called after me. "Keep away from Caleb. The boy's a brute. He broke our last stable lad's arm in a fight."

"Then you shouldn't have sent him to wake me up, should you!" I snapped, almost running out of the arched carriage gate and away from the stable yard.

At least Sid had brought my boots from the loft.

I nearly stomped right up the steps to the front door of the big house. Then I remembered servants were not allowed in that way. I squelched around the side of the kitchens to the service yard with the laundry at the back.

If the stables were cold and draughty, the laundry room was like an oven. There were steaming tubs everywhere with fires blazing to keep the water hot and heat the heavy smoothing irons to flatten the sheets. No wonder us stable boys were only given blankets. I had never thought before of all the work it took to wash and press fresh linen for the master and his family to sleep in every night.

"Excuse me," I shouted over the noise of a grinding mangle wringing water from a tablecloth. "James sent me from the stables. . ."

At the mention of his name, two rosy-faced girls began to giggle.

"James Howard sent you, did he?"

They bustled me into a side room, more like a cupboard full of folded sheets, but at least it was quiet enough to talk.

If it hadn't been eight o'clock in the morning, I would have thought the girls had been in the cider press and were drunk already, the way they were giggling and nudging each other.

"Did James have his sleeves rolled up?" asked one of them.

"His sleeves?"

"I wish he'd come up 'ere 'imself. You tell 'im, Daisy is 'ere any time 'e needs 'er 'elp," giggled the blonde.

"And Doris," said the darker one. "In fact, you give him this and say it was from me." She leant forward and smacked a big wet kiss right in the middle of my cheek.

Ugh. Whatever was the matter with them?

"If you'd smile a bit, you're not so bad-looking yourself," said Doris, crouching down in front of me. "Give it a couple of years and I might even dance with you at the harvest supper."

"Listen, all I need is some dry clothes," I said, sticking out my chin and scowling.

"All right, keep your shirt on... In fact, you better take it off before you die of cold." Daisy giggled.

"Take it off? Here? In front of you?" I folded my arms tight across my chest. "I – I can't do that."

"What do think we are? A couple of peeping

Toms?" said Doris scornfully. "Of course not here. Get behind that screen and we'll have your long johns too."

"Oh my lord! What have we here?" Wilf was halfway between the muck heap and the garden. He dropped his wheelbarrow and gaped at me with his mouth wide open.

I was not surprised he was staring. Daisy and Doris had dressed me up in a frilly white nightdress with my bare legs poking out of the bottom and my heavy working boots underneath.

"It's – it's one of Miss Jessie's from the big house," I blushed. "The girls in the laundry said there wasn't anything else."

"Hmm. Expect you rubbed them up the wrong way," said Wilf, serious for a moment. "I reckon you're a nice lad, Joe. Really I do. But you got to watch out for that. You can't fight with everyone you meet."

He was looking at me with his head on one side just like Nanny Clay used to when I threw a tantrum.

I was about to tell him to keep his nose out when his brother came down the path the other way.

"Good golly!" Sid giggled, grabbing me by the hand and waltzing me round and round Wilf's wheelbarrow. "Ain't you a pretty one, Joe lad?"

I knew he was only having fun but my cheeks burned bright red. If they carried on like this, I was worried they would find out I really was a girl. . .

I tried to pull free but Sid only let go when James appeared in the archway.

"Look at young Joe, here!" cried Wilf. "Doesn't he look like a proper girl?"

James surveyed me in silence then nodded his head. "I suppose he does."

He walked past us, heading in the direction of the laundry.

"Get up to the loft, Joe, and stay there till your own clothes are dry," he said, over his shoulder. "We don't need this kind of carnival in the stables."

I scrambled up the ladder. Sitting on my straw mattress, all alone in the silly frilly nightdress, my cheeks still burned with shame. I wanted to cry. But I'd promised myself I wouldn't.

Everyone at Birtwick was either furious with me or laughing in my face. As far as being a stable boy, I had made a total mess of that. James was right. It was a carnival . . . and I was the fool. I had barely even been allowed near a horse since I had ridden Black Beauty. All I had done was sweep the yard and carry hay.

Still – I'd show them! I'd be the finest stable lad Birtwick Park had ever seen.

Chapter Fourteen

By the time the laundry girls finally sent my dry things back, it was mid-afternoon.

Yet again, my stomach rumbled with hunger. I had missed lunch and nobody had thought to send any food up to me in the loft.

I stomped down the ladder, pleased to be in my stable lad's clothes again and making an extra point to swing my arms like a boy.

"Right, you can start there," said James, pointing to the stable with three little stalls where Merrylegs was tied up and Black Beauty had his big loose box. James handed me a leather bucket full of brushes and combs. "Groom all four until they shine. There's Beauty and Merrylegs. Justice the old cob. And

Ginger too – watch yourself around her; she has a quick temper sometimes."

"Grooming?" I'd hoped I'd be exercising the horses. I dreamed of nothing except riding Beauty since that first moment in the field.

"Yes, grooming," said James. "Unless you're too grand, of course. Did you never brush a horse at Summer's Place?"

"Er, yes, of course I did," I said quickly. In truth, I had never groomed a horse in my whole life. Old Thomas or one of the stable boys had always done that for me. But at least it was a step up from sweeping the yard.

I glanced around the stable. Black Beauty was already gleaming from where James had groomed him last night. Justice's cobby, roan coat looked too thick to ever shine. And although Ginger was a brilliant bronzed chestnut, she raised her back heel and flattened her ears as soon as I stepped near her stall.

Was that really how bad tempered the boys thought I was?

"You first then, Merrylegs," I said stepping quickly sideways to avoid Ginger and patting his dappled rump as I squeezed in beside him. I had brushed

Merrylegs's mane and tail at home before, just for fun, often plaiting it in the same way I played with Jemima and Arabella, my dolls.

I began there now, running a wide metal comb through his coarse grey hair. When his mane was tangle-free and his tail was as bushy as a fox, I stood back to admire my work.

Perfect! Then I brushed his neck and back, especially the big dapple spots on his rump. There was a strange hooked thing in the bucket but I had no idea what that was for. Perhaps to clean the brushes? But there was a jar of oil and a thick brush like an artist would use. I knew this was to oil his hooves.

"There!" I said, kissing the end of his nose. "Just wait until the young ladies of the house see you." I'd been told they were away for a few days but would return tomorrow. "They'll say you're the smartest pony in the whole of Birtwick Park." He was the only pony, of course. Even Justice was over fourteen hands. But I didn't tell him that.

I was very proud of the way Merrylegs looked, but knew that if I wanted prove to everyone that I was a proper stable boy, it would have to be difficult Ginger I tackled next.

"Good girl, steady now!" I said, slipping in to the stall beside her.

When James found me, I was pressed up against the manger in the back of Ginger's stall. Her ears were flat and she would not let me past her to escape.

"Look!" I cried, holding up my arm. "She bit me. Hard." There were spots of blood seeping through the clean white cotton of my shirt.

"We've only had her here six weeks," said James, squeezing in beside me. He patted Ginger's flank, whispering to her gently as he edged past. "She bit me on her first day too." He pointed to a scar above his elbow. (Doris and Daisy would be pleased to know his sleeves were indeed rolled up.)

"You should sell her," I said sulkily. "Six weeks is long enough to learn her lesson. What's the point in keeping a bad-tempered mare who can't be tamed?"

The pain was throbbing in my arm.

"Perhaps you're right," said James. He let Ginger nuzzle her nose in his palm. She seemed as calm as Merrylegs now, with her ears pricked forward showing off her pretty head. "I reckon we'll try her with kindness for a little longer first," he said. "She's had a hard life so far. The dealer who sold her told Mr Manly said she had been poorly treated and badly beaten at her last home."

"That's terrible," I said, feeling calmer now. "I can't understand why anyone would be cruel to an animal."

James nodded, patting Ginger and pushing her gently to one side so we could pass. "Go back into the stall and give her some oats," he said. "Just a little handful, mind. Not so much as to spoil her, but enough to show you want to be her friend."

I was nervous to go back inside alone. But, sure enough, Ginger let me pass without a fuss. She ate the oats from my hand and, although she did not nuzzle me when they were finished, she kept her ears pricked forward all the time.

"You were right!" I beamed as I stepped out of the stall.

But James was frowning at me with his hands on his hips.

"What have you been doing all this time?" he asked. "Justice is not groomed yet."

"Well. . ." I stammered.

"And Beauty is not groomed either," he said.

"Er. . ." I'd hoped he wouldn't notice that. He'd

made Beauty's black coat gleam like a raven's wing himself last night.

"And the pony?" He spun around and looked at Merrylegs. "Why is he only half done?"

"Half done? I spent over an hour. He's perfect," I cried.

But James was already leading Merrylegs out of his stall into the light.

"Look at this," he said. It was true. The oil was patchy on his hooves. I could see that now.

"And here?" He ran a hand along Merrylegs's belly. "You've only brushed his top and sides but underneath he's caked with mud."

"Ha!" I half laughed, hoping James was joking. Although I should have known better by now. "What does it matter if he's not clean underneath? Nobody will see it there."

"It matters," said James, "because Miss Flora and Miss Jessie will want to ride their new pony tomorrow. If he has dirt under his belly it will rub against his girth and make him sore."

"Oh. . ." I had never known that. I thought horses were groomed just to make them pretty.

"And his hooves!" James lifted Merrylegs's feet. "You haven't cleaned them out. He picked up the strange hook thing from amongst the brushes. "What's the matter with you, Joe Green? Have you never seen a hoof pick before?"

"A hoof pick?" So that is what the funny object was. "Of course I have," I lied. And I did remember now that one of the stable lads would always lift our horses' feet before Father or I went out for a ride.

"It is your job to look after this pony," James said. "Mr Manly and the master may think you are a fine horseman and perhaps you can ride passably well, but you know nothing about how to care for a horse. Nothing at all."

"Fine! I'll clean out his hooves!" I snatched to take the pick from James's hand but he thrust a pitchfork at me instead.

"You can do the mucking out," he growled. "That should keep you busy until you learn how things are done around here."

"You mean, I'm not allowed to work with the horses at all? I won't get to ride them?"

"Ride them?" James laughed. "You can muck them out and clean their tack. If you learn how to do that properly, I might just let you lead one around the yard. But I wouldn't raise your hopes. Not before Christmas."

He pointed to a steaming pile of dung Merrylegs had left on the cobbles. "Get started. You'll need a broom and shovel too."

I watched as he led Merrylegs away.

I was fuming. I wanted to hurl the pitchfork on the ground. But what James had said was right. I could ride a horse but I had no idea how to care for one. Was I spoiled? Had I been spoiled all my life?

"Tough day?" asked Sid, appearing behind me with the wheelbarrow. He was on one of his endless trips between the muck heap and the kitchen garden where they used the horse manure to help the vegetables grow. "Chuck that in here if you like." He pointed to the pile of dung I had shovelled up and I threw it in his barrow.

"Thank you." I tried to smile.

Sid was right. It had been a tough day. James thought I was useless. And I'd made an enemy of Caleb. But I had found friends too, I think. Although Sid and Wilf liked to tease and joke, they were kind. And the horses were wonderful. There was Merrylegs, of course. And I had almost made a friend of Ginger. But it was Beauty who leant over his loose box door, watching me wherever I went. He whinnied softly now as if he understood how unhappy and foolish James's harsh words had made me feel. As we looked at each other, my spirits lifted. I knew there was something special – a connection between us. I'd felt it the very first moment I saw him – as if, after everything I'd lost, Beauty had come into my life for a reason. It was as if I had come here to Birtwick specially to find him.

I made myself a promise, there and then. No matter how hard the work was, or how difficult pretending to be a boy became, I would stay here and get to know Black Beauty better. Maybe one day, I would even get to ride him again.

Chapter Fifteen

As spring turned into summer at Birtwick Park, things did slowly begin to get better. I worked hard and it was not long before I could harness a horse, pick its hooves and make a bran mash. Caleb called me "Slow Joe" because all my tasks took so long at first. But Mr Manly said, "Better done well than done hasty." As I grew stronger, I could shovel as much muck as lazy Caleb, for all his muscles and showing off. While he was rough with the horses, I was gentle.

Caleb didn't sleep in the loft with us at night. He stayed alone in a little stone bothy at the bottom of the kitchen garden.

"He says it is because he snores," Sid explained.

"Which he does," said Wilf.

"But really, it is so he can slip out at night and go poaching with his friends from the village," said Sid.

I didn't care if Caleb slept in the pigsty just so long as he kept away from me. I dropped exhausted on my mattress at the end of each day and slept like a hibernating bear at night. My pale skin was more freckled than ever, speckled all over like a hen's egg from the sun. But I was happy. Happier perhaps than I had ever been. I loved being with the horses all day – even Ginger let me groom her now without a fuss – and I liked hard work and keeping busy.

Every once in a while I would think of Aunt Lavinia and The Slug. The first few times I saw a smart carriage pull up at the front of the big house, my heart would leap into my mouth at the thought it might be someone sent to fetch me back, guessing perhaps that I had come with Merrylegs to his new home. But I soon stopped worrying. Maybe Aunt Lavinia would just tell people I had gone to be a companion to Lady Hexham as they planned. After all, the old lady was a recluse. Nobody would have any idea if I was there or not. And who would ask anyway? Only my dear old Nanny Clay, and she was in Fairstowe, the pretty-sounding village, with her nephew.

It was a good thing Nanny Clay couldn't see me now. I'd had to trim my hair again to keep it short above my ears like a boy. But so far I had remained undiscovered. There had been one dreadful sunny afternoon when Wilf and Sid wanted me to go bathing in the lake; I'd thought they would drag me there, but in the end I managed to convince them I was sick and escape back to the loft. Most evenings, while the others washed themselves in the water trough, I sneaked away to a stream at the bottom of the orchard. They decided I was shy and teased me mercilessly, but I was getting better and better at passing myself off as a boy. Perhaps, where I gained my love of horses from Father, I had inherited a little acting skill from Mother too.

One morning, I spread my feet apart and swaggered over to the churn stand. I took a gulp of milk, drinking straight from the pail, and belched as loudly as any real stable lad ever could.

I turned around, expecting the boys to laugh, thinking I was one of them. But James was furious.

"Watch your manners," he growled. "This is a stable, not the gutter."

Perhaps belching like a bullfrog was going a little too far . . . even for a boy.

"Now go and saddle Merrylegs," said James. "Miss Jessie and Miss Flora want to ride him in the orchard this morning. You can keep an eye on them while you're mucking out the stables. Mr Manly has gone to Newmarket for a few days to see about a new mare. He asked me to run Justice down to the village on an errand with the cart."

"Yes. Right away," I said still blushing from my enormous belch and pleased that gentle Mr Manly hadn't been here to witness it too.

"And clean the side-saddle," James added. "I am told the mistress may wish to take Beauty out later."

"Really?" I raised an eyebrow. The mistress of the house was a great source of fascination for me; Black Beauty belonged to her but she had become ill recently and had not been seen outside.

"Doctor White was here yesterday and I believe there has been some improvement," said James.

I was pleased. I'd only met the mistress once or twice but she seemed kind. And I liked Squire Gordon more and more. I also liked their children, Miss Jessie and Miss Flora. Although I had been jealous at first, I had to admit they adored Merrylegs and he was fond of them too.

Miss Jessie, the eldest, was still a few years younger than me and little Flora's stirrups barely reached the bottom of the saddle when she was riding the tubby pony. They were both more suited to Merrylegs than I would be now – especially as I had grown half a head taller since the spring. Billy's trousers now fitted me well.

As soon as Merrylegs saw the girls coming towards the yard, he whinnied with excitement.

"Traitor!" I whispered, patting his neck. But really I was just pleased he was happy and busy, as we both were at Birtwick Park.

"Darling pony!" Miss Jessie held out a sugar lump and paid no attention to me, holding Merrylegs's bridle. I couldn't blame her. I still blushed with shame when I thought how I hadn't known Billy the stable boy's name back when I had been grand Miss Josephine at Summer's Place.

Little Flora was different though.

"Good morning, Merrylegs," she cried, standing on tiptoes to throw her arms around his neck. "Good morning, Joe." She grinned up at me, showing the gap where she had lost her baby teeth. "Did Merrylegs snore in the night again?"

"Most dreadfully! Like a roaring dragon." I sighed. It was a joke we always shared.

"You are lucky, Joe," she said, as I helped Miss Jessie mount. "I wish I could be a boy. Then I could sleep above the stables every night."

"You never know!" I grinned. "Perhaps one day you will. . ."

"Don't be ridiculous!" Miss Jessie clicked her tongue to tell Merrylegs to walk on. "It wouldn't matter if you were a boy or a girl, Flora. You would have to be a servant to sleep out here in the yard. And you wouldn't want that, would you?"

She still didn't look at me as she gathered her reins and trotted towards the orchard.

"I wouldn't mind anything as long as I could always be with Merrylegs," whispered Flora, slipping her hand into mine as we followed under the arch. "Pay no attention to Jess. She is just in a bad mood because our cousin Aubrey is here. He is a boy. A horrid one. . ."

"Oh dear. Cousins can be like that," I said.

"He's been trying to shoot the doves out of the nursery window," explained Flora. "And he says he wants to ride Merrylegs later on."

Flora was right. Aubrey was not a nice boy. He came down to the yard just as I was untacking

Merrylegs after the girls had ridden him in the orchard for an hour. Jessie had gone back to the house but I had given little Flora a comb and she was plaiting Merrylegs's tail.

"Take that silly girl thing off," cried Aubrey pointing to the little side-saddle. "And fetch something a man can ride with!"

A man? He didn't look a day older than me and he was thin as a ferret.

"Do you wish to go for a ride, Master Aubrey?" I asked politely.

"Yes. Hurry up and saddle this fat little thing!" He slapped his hand hard on Merrylegs's rump.

"Perhaps we can find you something more suitable," I said. "Merrylegs has already been out with the young ladies this morning."

"He is dreadfully tired," agreed Flora.

"And you are perhaps a little tall and strong for him. He is a child's pony," I said, hoping to appeal to Aubrey's pride. Justice was still out in the village with James but I spotted Caleb leading the black and white farm cob in from the field.

"Perhaps Badger would suit?" I said, pointing to the piebald. He was a steady old thing of fourteen hands and had taken Miss Flora's friends often.

"For me?" Aubrey snorted. "I wouldn't be seen dead on a fat painted nag like that. It is only fit to be ridden by gypsies and drovers!"

"Ooh! I wish I was a gypsy." Flora clapped her hands with excitement. "Merrylegs would have a brightly coloured wagon and we would trot along the lanes all day. You could come too if you liked, Joe. At night we would make a fire and. . ."

"Shut up! Why don't you go back to the nursery?" snarled Aubrey.

I wished I could say something . . . or better still, toss him head first into the muck heap. But as a servant, the best I could do was smile kindly at Flora and wait for Aubrey to give me my orders.

He glanced around the yard as if checking for something better than Merrylegs after all. Luckily I had just filled Black Beauty's hay rack and he was in the back of his loose box where he could not be seen or I am sure the boy would have wanted to take the fine horse out at once. But Ginger was looking out of her stall.

"How about that one?" Aubrey took a step forward. Ginger laid her ears flat against her head as if sensing danger. It was something I had not seen her do for many weeks now.

"Perhaps not!" Aubrey darted behind Merrylegs. He was obviously a coward as well as a bully. "I asked you to prepare this fat pony ten minutes ago," he said, clicking his fingers at me. "What is keeping you, boy?"

"Sorry, Master Aubrey. I will be right back." I turned towards the tack room to fetch a different saddle for Merrylegs.

"And bring me a whip while you are at it!" cried Aubrey.

My heart sank. Poor Merrylegs. But what could I do? I was just a servant.

Chapter Sixteen

The odd thing was, by the time I came out from the back of the tack room carrying a saddle for Merrylegs, the pegs where we kept the whips and riding crops were quite empty.

"How very strange," I said loudly as I heard a rustle and saw a small blonde figure disappear behind a horse blanket hanging on the wall. "I think the rats and mice have been here. But whatever do they want with all our whips?"

There was a little giggle.

"Ah! I think I hear them squeaking," I said.

The giggle grew louder.

"I shall have to send in the terriers later," I said with a great sigh. "Perhaps I will ask kind Miss Flora to lend me Frisky." He was her own little dog. "But for now I must hurry out and tell Master Aubrey that a dreadful thing has happened and no whips can be found."

"Ridiculous. What sort of stable has no whips?" snarled Aubrey.

"You may check for yourself if you like," I said, seeing Flora slip out of the tack room door.

"It is true," she called. "There is not a whip in there. Mother will not allow it." Her eyes grew wide as she added to the story. "The thought of a horse being beaten makes her feel quite ill. . ."

"No wonder she is always in her bed," muttered Aubrey under his breath. "I never heard anything so silly!"

"Don't worry. You won't need a whip to make Merrylegs get going," I assured him as he mounted. "He is much more spirited than he looks."

"We shall see about that," said Aubrey, kicking his legs so hard I heard them slap against the saddle. He yanked Merrylegs's head around until half the bit was out of the side of his mouth.

"Careful!" I begged. But Aubrey did not hear me. He was too busy shouting at Merrylegs to "Giddy up!".

I still had Beauty's side-saddle to clean for the mistress, but every time I lifted the blacking on my cloth Flora tugged at my sleeve.

"Go out to the lane, Joe," she begged me. "Go and see if Merrylegs is coming back. Check that he is all right."

"I have to polish this saddle for your mother first," I said. Although inside, I was as worried as Flora and kept glancing out into the yard, listening anxiously for the sound of Merrylegs's little hooves on the stones.

"Mother won't mind," said Flora, tugging my sleeve again.

"Maybe not. But James will," I said.

At last the saddle was gleaming. I knew I should whiten the linen girth as well but it was already spotless. When Flora tugged at my sleeve again, I gave in.

"Come on, then!" I said. We ran up the steep lane. But, as we passed the orchard, I saw that Aubrey had taken Merrylegs in there.

"What is he doing?" I asked.

The boy was galloping Merrylegs up towards the high gate in the far corner and then back again. He had taken a long thin hazel stick from the hedge and was using that as a home-made whip to thrash poor Merrylegs with.

How dare he?

"Wait here!" I told Flora as I dashed between the trees.

"Stop that at once, Aubrey!" I cried. I did not care who was servant and who was master now. He could not beat my poor little pony like that.

"Get back!" he roared, lashing the whip at me. "This stupid brute will not obey me."

"Obey you?" What was he trying to make Merrylegs do? He had already spun him around and galloped away again. Then I saw the plan.

Aubrey was trying to make Merrylegs jump the gate. It was uphill and quite impossible. Even Black Beauty could not have made a leap like that.

"Damn you, Merryfoot, jump!" roared Aubrey.

"His name is Merrylegs and you mustn't beat him," wailed Flora running towards us.

"Keep back," I warned her as Merrylegs swerved sideways and slithered down the hill. No matter how hard Aubrey whipped him, he knew he would break his legs if he tried to make the jump; this could only end in danger for one or both of them. I *had* to stop this. Catching hold of the reins, I pulled them to a halt. Aubrey's face was a mask of astonishment.

"What on earth – what on earth do you think you're doing? Out of my way, stable boy."

"No! You must not make Merrylegs take that jump." I made my voice very loud and firm, to quell the nerves I felt inside. This could cost me my job – but I had to say something. "It is too difficult a jump for any horse, let alone a little pony. Please, you mustn't try it."

For a moment, Aubrey just stared at me, and then with a sudden wrench he yanked the reins out of my grasp and turned Merrylegs. I gasped as the reins tore through my hands, and stumbled, nearly falling.

"How dare you!" Aubrey was thin and wiry, but he was strong. Although Merrylegs was bucking now, he pulled his head around again and galloped him back up the hill.

Clever Merrylegs had plans of his own. He charged forward as if he was going to take the jump at last. Then he skidded to a stop and thrust his head between his legs.

Aubrey flew through the air. For a moment I thought he would shoot right over the gate itself but he landed head first in the thorny hedge.

"Help!" From the way that he was wriggling and thrashing about, I could see that nothing was broken; only his stupid pride was hurt. "Get me out of here," he cried.

But I ignored him. We all did.

Merrylegs was already nibbling grass and swishing his tail as if nothing had happened, while Flora fussed around the little pony and kissed his ears.

"You poor darling," she cried.

"Come on, trouble!" I patted him too as I took hold of the reins. Then I saw the long thin hazel whip lying on the ground. I picked it up and broke it over my knee.

"You won't be needing that again," I said, leaving Aubrey still bellowing upside down in the hedge.

We began to walk down through the orchard when I gasped; James was standing there with his hands on his hips. I didn't even know he was back from the village yet. The squire was beside him.

They were both frowning, with faces like thunder.

My heart, already leaping in my chest, began to pound. This was it. Of all the foolish things I had done since arriving at Birtwick Park, this had to be the worst. I had left the squire's nephew buried in a thorny hedge without even trying to get him out. It didn't matter that he had been cruel and stupid and mean. It didn't even matter that he had put Merrylegs's life at risk. I would be dismissed and sent on my way. The squire would have to teach me a lesson and James would do nothing to defend me.

"Daddy!" Flora ran into her father's arms. "You mustn't be cross with Joe," she cried. "Or with Merrylegs. Aubrey was being a pig. He was beating Merrylegs and trying to make him do an impossible jump."

"Well," the squire looked at me over the top of her blonde head, "while I'm sure it would have been better to help the young man out of the hedge – and, Flora, you really must not call your cousin a pig – we saw everything that happened. And no, I am not cross. At least not with Merrylegs ... or with Joe."

"You're not?" I couldn't help but gasp out loud.

"No. That is no way to treat a horse and it looks like Aubrey needed to learn a lesson," said Squire Gordon, as we saw the boy trudging down the orchard towards us. Leaves and twigs were still sticking out of his hair and coat and he was crimson with shame. "I don't think he will ride like that again."

When Aubrey reached us, the squire turned his stern face on the boy. "Through your foolhardy riding, young man, you have put poor Joe here in a fix; he had to choose between disobeying you or protecting the pony." Aubrey scowled. "Shake hands with him and apologize."

"Sorry!" Aubrey grunted and stared at his boots, grudgingly putting his hand in mine. He tried to pull away again almost at once. But I did not let go. I kept my head held high until he was forced to lift his eyes and look up at me.

"I do not need an apology," I said. "But you should say you are sorry to Merrylegs."

"Yes!" cried Flora, darting forward and pummelling her fists against her cousin's chest. "You will never ride him ever, ever, ever, ever again."

When we were back in the yard I thought that James would scold me for sure.

Instead, he handed me Black Beauty's bridle.

"I will settle Merrylegs. You go and tack up Beauty," he said gruffly.

"For the mistress?" I asked.

"No. For you. The mistress is still unwell. Beauty will need exercise."

"You mean ... you want me to ride him? You want me to ride Black Beauty?" I gasped.

"Don't look so surprised. You ride well, even if it is all wild circus tricks!" James smiled at me and his grey eyes lit up.

I glowed with pride.

"You did right to protect Merrylegs today, Joe," he said. "Good work."

Chapter Seventeen

I couldn't believe it. My heart was in my throat and my whole body was shaking with excitement. I was about to ride Black Beauty.

James held Beauty's head while I mounted. It was the only part of riding like a boy I had any difficulty with, but I put my foot in the stirrup and sprang on board as lightly as I could.

Beauty danced and pranced and shook himself.

"He's been shut inside too long," said James. "Go up by the common and the highwood, then back by the watermill and the river. That should take the tickle out of his feet."

"Thank you!" I couldn't believe I was actually riding Beauty again at long last. "I'll take him slowly to start with," I promised.

James nodded. I knew he would be watching me from the yard and I longed to prove to him there was more to my riding than what he called "circus tricks".

I made Beauty walk as we passed under the archway and along the drive. He swished his tail and played with his bit. He was still prancing as we passed the gatehouse but I wouldn't let him trot. I wanted Beauty to get used to the feeling of me in the saddle. He needed to sense that I was in charge of him and calm – this would be no wild bareback gallop today.

Then, as soon as we were through the village, I squeezed my legs and let Beauty go on up the lane at a spanking trot. It was wonderful to hear his hooves on the ground and fall into a natural rising rhythm with his stride. But, as he twitched his ears at the brow of the hill, I knew we were both desperate for a sight of the common and the soft earth where we could gallop at last.

Riding bareback had been an exhilarating adventure, but galloping with a saddle was even better. We were in control, like one person – horse and rider – joined together. At first we went flat out, then slowed to a canter past the highwood. Flat out again until we saw the watermill, and trotted slowly home along the river.

"Welcome back," said James as we walked calmly into the yard. He laid his hand on the Beauty's neck and listened to his breathing. "Well done," he said, nodding approvingly. "You have worked him well, but rested him properly and not tired him out."

"He was fleet as a deer," I cried, leaning forward to throw my arms around Beauty's neck. "The lightest touch of the rein and he turned. The tiniest squeeze of my leg and he was off."

James shook his head and laughed. "You enjoyed it then?" he said. But, for the first time, I did not feel he was teasing me or telling me off. He knew what I meant.

"You can take him out again tomorrow, if the mistress is still unwell," he said. "If the master doesn't ride I will join you on Ginger."

As I carried the fine French saddle back to the tack room, it seemed to weigh no more than a feather. I wanted to throw it up in the air and turn a cartwheel. I wanted to shout so loud that everyone in the big house would hear me.

I had ridden the most beautiful horse in all the

world and James Howard thought I had done it well.

It was a fine afternoon and, after a quick rub down, James decided to let Beauty have a graze in the home paddock with Justice, Merrylegs and Ginger.

We stood leaning on the gate and watched them for a while as they scratched each other's necks and swished their tails under the trees.

For a long time neither of us said anything. Then James shook himself as if he had been lost in a dream.

"It would break my heart if ever I couldn't be around horses," he said.

"Me too," I agreed.

I realized suddenly that it was true; with my father dead and my mother lost to me, this was what really mattered now. Horses – and especially the wonderful Black Beauty.

The mistress had not improved by the following morning and James and I did take Ginger and Beauty out for a ride together. It was fun to watch the horses prick their ears and trot along side by side. Ginger was quite used to Beauty from the stables and didn't try to nip him or bite.

The next day was the same and James even let us race the horses at a gallop on the common. Beauty and I won by a nose. James said I should have gone away to Newmarket with Mr Manly to see if I could be a jockey, I was so small and light.

I felt proud as anything and only boasted a *little* to the twins about my victory when we all settled down to sleep in the loft that night.

It seemed my eyes had only been closed for a moment when we were woken by a terrible shouting from down below. The stable bell was ringing and a footman had come running from the house.

"Wake up! Wake up!" he cried. "James Howard, come quick! The master needs you."

James leapt to his feet and we all hurried down the ladder.

"You must take this note to the doctor," said the footman. "It is from the squire. The mistress has taken a turn for the worse and you must bring help at once."

James took the note and scrambled back up to the loft to pull on his coat and breeches. "I'll go this minute," he called. "Joe, saddle Beauty for me. He is the fastest horse we have. It is a fair gallop to Doctor

White's house. Eight miles at least..."

The twins held a lantern each as I dashed into the tack room to grab a saddle and bridle and then to Beauty's stall.

"I'll push Beauty to his limits and then take the journey home more slowly," said James, as we worked frantically to tack him. "The doctor will come on his own bay mare; make sure she is made comfortable, Joe."

"I will," I promised.

"Good luck, James." Wilf glanced at the sky. "At least there's a bright moon so you can see where you're going."

"Hurry," said Sid.

I stretched out my hand to touch Black Beauty's nose but before I could reach him, James had turned the horse's head and galloped away.

"Take care!" I called, but my words were lost in the wind.

Chapter Eighteen

Half the estate seemed to be awake that night. Lamplight flickered in the windows of the big house.

The only person missing from the commotion was Caleb and we all knew where he was on such a bright moonlit night – poaching in the wood.

Two hours ticked by. The twins dozed. I paced up and down. I even groomed Merrylegs by lamplight just to pass the time.

Then I heard it.

Hooves on the driveway. The gatekeeper shouted, "Hello!"

I dashed out to grab the horse by the bridle so the doctor could go straight to the house, when I saw that it was not the bay mare he was riding; it was Beauty.

"My own horse is lame," puffed the doctor. He was a heavy man with a belly like a beer barrel. "I took this fellow and he did you proud."

Poor Beauty was dripping with sweat.

"Your lad James is coming back by foot," grunted the doctor as he heaved himself out of the saddle. "I reckon he will be some time."

Then the doors were flung open and he disappeared inside the house.

Beauty's legs were shaking so much I could barely lead him to the stable.

"We'll take a couple of horses and ride out and meet James," said Sid, slipping a halter on Justice as his brother ran to fetch Badger.

The two boys both clambered on to the big piebald cob. Sid held out his arm, leading Justice behind them for James to ride home.

"I don't know much about nags," said Wilf, kicking his heels. "But poor Beauty looks fit to boil."

"Like a pot on fire," said Sid.

"Please. Be quick!" I begged as they trotted away. I knew Beauty was in a terrible state and I desperately wanted James to come back and tell me what to do.

But for now I was alone. I would just have to manage the best I could.

I flung open the loose box door and led Beauty inside. The boys were right. The poor thing was as hot as a stove. I grabbed a cloth and began to rub his chest. There wasn't a dry hair on his body, sweat ran down his legs and steam rose up from his back.

His sides were heaving and he hung his head and made a deep panting sound from his throat.

"Oh, Beauty. What do I do?" I cried. It could be another hour before James and the twins were back. If only Mr Manly wasn't still away at Newmarket. Even if Caleb was here that would be something...

I had no idea what was best to do for a horse as hot as this. I tried to think what old Thomas would have done when I was still living at Summer's Place. There must have been a hundred times I had brought Merrylegs home lathered with sweat, his flanks heaving as he puffed like a bull. In truth, of course, I had no inkling what Thomas would have done. Hard as I tried, all I could remember was the nod of his head as he took hold of my pony's bridle and led him away. "Very good, Miss Josephine, I'll make this fellow nice and comfy," he would say as I dashed inside for a soak in the tub and a glass of barley water with Nanny Clay.

"I know one thing, if you're hot, we must get you cool," I said to Beauty, dashing to the pump to fetch a bucket of cold water.

"There!" He plunged his nose and drank greedily. "I'll get you another." Then I flung open the big window at the back of the loose box. "That will let some nice cold air in," I said.

I ran my hand over his back; the water seemed to have settled him a little. I decided to feed him too and gave him a scoop of corn and some fresh hay.

"That's better, isn't it?" I said. It was common sense. Black Beauty was hot and tired. Now I had cooled him down and fed him. Surely that was the right thing to do.

I shut the loose box door so Beauty could rest and went to get a drink of water for myself. Merrylegs whinnied.

"Greedy boy," I said. But I fetched him and Ginger a pile of hay. Then I filled a rack for Justice to have when he got back. There was no sign of anyone yet.

I took some hay to Badger's stall and glanced up the road.

Still nothing.

I wondered back and popped my head over the loose box door.

Black Beauty was lying on the floor. His sides were heaving like bellows.

"Beauty? What's the matter?" I flung open the door and knelt beside the shivering horse. He lifted his neck and tried to look at me, but his eyes rolled and his head dropped back to the straw.

He let out a long low moan and then kicked his legs wildly. I leapt out of the way.

He shivered and thrashed as if there were demons inside his belly.

"Shh! Beauty, steady." I stretched out my hand trying to get close. But my heart was thumping. There was nothing I could do.

Then, at last, he was still. So still I thought he might be dead.

I crawled close and laid my head against his side. He was still breathing but his eyes were closed.

I jumped to my feet again and began to pace. Why wasn't James back yet? Or Caleb, damn him?

Should I run to the house and fetch the squire? Would he know what to do to save Beauty?

I was halfway to the door.

But no. What if his wife was dying?

I shouldn't disturb them.

I turned back . . . then spun around again.

I must go. I must fetch help.

The mistress had the doctor. He would do all he could for her. Black Beauty had nobody. Only me.

And I was useless.

I was on the drive, pelting towards the house when I heard the thud of Justice's hooves thundering through the gate.

"James!" I cried. "James, come quick. I think I have killed Black Beauty."

James leapt from Justice's back and dashed into the stable.

He took one look at the poor horse lying on the ground and grabbed a rug. He threw it over Beauty and then ran to fetch another blanket and warm gruel.

"Sid," he barked as the twins rode into the yard. "Run up to the house and fetch me some hot water. You too, Wilf."

He did not ask me to do anything. He did not even look at me. All I could do was tie up the cobs and open and close the loose box door as James dashed back and forth to fetch straw and hot cloths.

"Stupid, stupid boy," he muttered under his breath.

I know now that instead of trying to cool Beauty down, I should have kept him snug.

Instead of buckets and buckets of cold water, I should have given him a little warm.

Instead of flinging open draughty windows, I should have covered him with blankets.

But I didn't know any of that. Not then.

At last, James sat back on his heels and began to stroke Beauty's nose.

I crept forward and knelt beside him.

"I'm so sorry. I tried my best," I stammered. "I just didn't. . ."

"Didn't what?" growled James.

I was too ashamed to raise my head but I could feel his angry grey eyes boring into me. All I could hear was the sound of Beauty's breathing, rasping as he gasped for breath.

"I – I didn't know what to do," I admitted.

"Then you have no business in a stable," said James. His voice was almost a whisper. I wish he had shouted at me and raged. As I lifted my head at last, I saw his back was turned again. He was bent over, gently stroking Beauty's head.

"Ignorance is as bad as wickedness when you have a horse's life in your hands," he said.

Chapter Nineteen

All that night, I stayed curled up next to Beauty on the straw. He was quiet and breathing more steadily now, but when Mr Manly came home from Newmarket in the morning he sent for the horse doctor right away.

"Will he die?" I cried, as the strange little man listened to Beauty's chest, poked him in the ribs and poured a draught of thick black medicine down his throat.

"Only time will tell," said the veterinarian. "But with rest and good care he may pull through."

For the next two weeks, I could hardly swallow my food, I felt so sick with worry. But I forced myself to eat and stay strong. I did my chores like lightning so I could spend every waking moment with Beauty. I wasn't allowed to sleep in his stable again but I got up four times every night to check that he was all right. James was keeping a good eye on him too, but we did not speak to each other. In all that time he barely said a word to me.

Flora came to tell us her mother was growing stronger. She lent me a book of fairy tales and I sat and read them to Beauty for hours after supper each day.

I knew he couldn't really understand, but I think he liked the sound of my voice. He would flick his ears and sigh as if listening to every word. Sometimes, when I paused, he would nudge my leg as if urging me to carry on.

"I am sure your favourite is Cinderella," I told him. "How handsome you would look pulling a golden pumpkin coach to the ball."

I thought the twins might laugh at me for reading to a horse. I wouldn't have cared if they did. But they seemed to understand I needed to be with Beauty and help him to grow strong and well again. Often, when I was reading, I would see them perched in Merrylegs's manger, listening too.

"Our old Ma used to tell us stories," said Sid.

"She can't read, but remembered them all by heart."
I knew the twins missed their mother dreadfully.
She lived about ten miles away on a smallholding
with a cider orchard and a flock of white geese. She
couldn't afford to keep the boys at home, not with
six brothers and sisters to feed.

"My favourite story is Dick Whittington," said
Wilf. "Lord Mayor of London! I should love to go to
the big city one day."

"My mother is in London," I said, a picture of her
face flashing into my mind. Then I remembered that
I had told everyone I was an orphan. "I mean, she
was there once," I added quickly. For all I knew she
might not be in London anyway by now. She could
be anywhere.

"Did she used to tell you stories?" asked Sid.

I shook my head and began to read another
tale. I had said too much already. But I did smile
as I saw that I had opened the page on the story
of Rapunzel, the girl who has all of her long hair
snipped short.

Even Caleb did not laugh at me for reading to
Black Beauty. Although he never came to listen
to the stories, I often found that he had cleaned
a harness I was set to do, filled a water trough or

mucked out a stable – extra things so I could hurry through my chores.

We both knew if he had been there the night the doctor came, he could have shown me how to tend to Beauty. I think he felt guilty – and grateful too. If Mr Manly knew he was poaching in the woods, Caleb would have lost his job and been up before the magistrate, probably sentenced to a spell in jail. But there was nothing to be gained by blaming him. He told everybody he had slept through it all. And I said nothing. I still felt the true fault lay with me.

For now, I was pleased to have Caleb's help with my work. It was good not to have him as an enemy. And he never called me "Slow Joe" again.

Only James did not come to hear the stories. He didn't even speak to me unless it was to give me an order and tell me what to do.

He was right to be angry. I had put Black Beauty's life in danger because I didn't know how to do my job properly. I wasn't a real stable boy; I was a pampered young girl who could ride well, but who didn't know anything about horses. I'd had servants to do the hard work and look after them for me all my life. And my play-acting had nearly killed Black Beauty. His fever had passed, but he was still weak. He spent most of his time lying on the stable floor.

Then at dawn one morning, as I came down from the loft to check on him as usual, something wonderful happened. Perhaps Beauty had been waiting for me. Perhaps I was a few minutes late. Either way, he raised his head, leapt to his feet and whinnied with delight. After that, the shine came back to his coat. He grew quite fat, as he was not ready for exercise yet, and his eyes were bright.

Another month passed, and now he whinnied again every time he saw me. If Beauty knew I had put him in danger, he never showed it. The bond between us was stronger than ever.

"A full recovery! I knew Beauty was a fighter," said Mr Manly leaning over the loose box door. "Yet, I don't think he'd have made it through without your care, Joe. You've done great work tending to him, lad. Well done."

"He never would have been ill in the first place if it wasn't for me," I choked.

"You don't know that," said Mr Manly kindly. "That gallop home with the doctor was enough to knock him sideways by itself."

"I just wish I had known the right thing to do," I said, rubbing Beauty's nose.

"Well, now you do and it's not a mistake you'll make again," said Mr Manly. "We'll shape you into a fine stable lad yet. You're learning fast, Joe."

"Thank you." For a moment I felt a warm glow, as though things might yet turn out right; but as I looked up I saw James walking past with a harness slung over his arm. He didn't even glance in our direction. He certainly didn't smile. I thought of what friends we had started to become when we used to ride Beauty and Ginger together on the common. Now that friendship was broken.

"I know he has been harsh with you," said Mr Manly, following my gaze. "It is only because he cares so much for the horses. You are more similar than you know."

"Similar? Me and James Howard? I don't think so!"

If I had my wish, I would have kept well out of James's way. But there was no avoiding him and a week or so later, we were thrown together again.

Squire Gordon brought the mistress to visit us in the yard. Although she was as thin as a sparrow and clung to the squire's arm, her cheeks were rosy and she laughed with delight when she saw Black Beauty up and well.

"The doctor says I would have died for sure if he had reached me even half an hour later," she said, stepping into the loose box.

She patted Black Beauty's neck. "By galloping like a demon you nearly killed yourself, but you saved my life. Thank you." She kissed his nose. "And thank you too." She turned and smiled at James. "I know you rode very bravely to fetch help."

"My pleasure, madam." James gave a little bow of his head.

"Oh, do not look so worried," teased the mistress. "I shall not kiss your nose like I did Black Beauty's."

James flushed scarlet. I couldn't help but giggle. He shot me an even sharper dagger-look than usual.

"You two will be busy these next few weeks," said the squire turning to us both. "I want you to exercise Ginger and get Beauty fit again so that my wife and I can ride together, just as soon as she is strong enough herself."

"Very good, sir." James did not look very happy at the thought spending time with me.

But I did not care about that. My heart leapt for joy.

I was going to ride Beauty again.

Chapter Twenty

Next morning, James and I got Ginger and Beauty ready for their first ride. We saddled the horses in silence but I couldn't stifle the huge grin as we set out.

We began by walking them to the watermill and back. Then trotting through the highwoods. At last we had a canter on the common.

Black Beauty swished his tail and bucked. I think he would have galloped flat out if I hadn't kept a tight hold on the reins.

"Whoa! Are you trying to throw me off?" I cried.

Black Beauty bucked again. I knew there was no meanness in it really. It was just that he was excited to feel well again and to be alive.

"Do you see that?" I said to James. "His spirit is as strong as ever."

"It is a wonderful thing!" James beamed.

I thought we might be friends again then. But when I talked about the haymaking or pointed to a cow and her calf, James only grunted and he was as stern and gruff as ever by the time we returned to the yard.

Fine! Let him be like that, I thought.

We rode most days, but barely shared a word. The mistress and Squire Gordon rode often too.

"Black Beauty is as strong as an ox again," said Mr Manly, one afternoon as they returned from a ride.

"I am pleased you think so too," agreed the squire. "Now my wife is well, we plan to visit her sister next week. It is a journey of over forty miles. Do you think Black Beauty will be up to taking us in the carriage with Ginger?"

"I don't doubt it for a moment," said Mr Manly, but a strange look passed over his face. "Next week, you say?"

"Yes." Squire Gordon did not seem to notice anything but the mistress dashed forward and patted Mr Manly's arm.

"Don't worry, Mr Manly, we will not need you with us," she said.

"Of course we shall need Manly. Who else will drive the carriage?" asked the squire in surprise.

"Mr Manly's wife is having a baby," said the mistress. "It is due next week. I am sure he will be anxious if he is so far from home."

"Oh no, madam! Do not trouble yourself." Poor Mr Manly blushed red as Ginger's coat.

"Good man. That's the spirit." The squire made to leave.

"Nonsense. I will not be persuaded," said the mistress. "You must stay here, Manly. James can drive the carriage and Joe can come along on the box seat. After all, nobody can manage Beauty as well as Joe can."

"That is true. Joe is a wonder with Beauty," said Mr Manly. "I never saw a horse and boy such friends. And James can drive the carriage just as well as any coachman." A little smile crept over his face and he blushed all over again. "If you are sure you could manage without me, then that would make Mrs Manly and myself very happy. It is our first child."

"Then that is settled!" said the mistress.

"As you wish, my dear," her husband agreed meekly.

The mistress clapped her hands. "How handsome you two young fellows will look on top of the carriage," she said, smiling at James and me. "I shall see about some new coats for you both."

"As you wish, my dear," sighed the squire.

"What's that?" I said, staring at the little green jacket with golden buttons which Doris had laid out for me on a bench in the laundry.

"It is your livery, silly. So you may look smart when you ride on the carriage," she said.

"James 'as one too. But I've taken 'is to the stable yard already," said Daisy. "I needed to be sure it was a good fit." She burst into fits of giggles which Doris didn't seem to find very funny at all.

"Hurry up, Joe. Are you going to try yours on or not?" she said, pulling me sharply by the ear.

"Ouch!" I yelped as she pushed me behind the little screen where I had got changed before.

"There's breeches too. As pale as cream. So don't go getting mucky fingermarks all over them," she said.

I have to admit, James and I did look very smart perched high on the gleaming carriage with Ginger and Beauty in their best black harness.

"Good luck!" Flora called up to me after she and Miss Jessie had said goodbye to their parents and the door of the carriage had been closed. "I do hope you don't meet any highwaymen."

"Oh, we are quite sure to!" I told her. "But don't worry, I will fight them with my sword."

"You don't have a sword, Joe!" Miss Jessie laughed.

"Oh yes, he does." Flora shook her head and looked very serious. "Before Joe decided to be a stable boy, he was going to be a pirate. He has a cutlass!"

"Ah-ha! Shiver me timbers!" I crowed, ignoring a sour look from James beside me.

"Gracious me!" Miss McKenzie, the girls' governess, began to look quite worried and ushered them back towards the house.

"Look after Merrylegs," I called.

"We will!" promised Flora. "The children from the vicarage are coming to ride with us this afternoon and they love Merry almost as much as we do."

"Have fun!" I cried over my shoulder.

James elbowed me in the ribs. Hard.

"Will you be quiet!" he hissed. "This is a gentleman's carriage not a fish wagon. You cannot sit up here and holler as if you were selling cockles and whelks on the shore."

"Fine!" I straightened my back and sat tall. I would never get used to how servants are meant to be so silent. It's always thought best when we don't say anything at all.

As it was, James and I were still not talking anyway and he had to concentrate on driving the big carriage up and down the hills. He seemed always to be fiddling and clicking his tongue and pulling on the reins to keep the horses in the centre of the road, well away from the ditches.

I had no real tasks, so sat on the box and admired the countryside. It was the first time I'd had no chores and nothing to do for a whole morning since I first arrived at Birtwick Park.

I sat back and smiled, letting the sun warm my face and thinking how I wouldn't swap the life of a stable boy for anything. Not now.

Chapter Twenty-one

We reached Riverford, the bustling market town where we were to spend the night, as the sun was going down. We stopped at a large hotel called the White Lion and dropped the master and mistress at the front, then we drove under an archway into a long yard with stables at one end and a coach house at the other.

There was an ostler in charge of the stable and a boy a year or two older than James who was supposed to help with the horses too.

"Step to it, Towler," cried the ostler. "Get those harnesses off."

"Right away," said the boy. But the minute the ostler's back was turned he leant against the wall.

"I'll just finish my smoke," he said with a nod to

us. I'm sure if Mr Manly had been there he would have leapt forward straight away. He sighed and made a great show of puffing and blowing into his clay pipe instead.

"How far have you come?" he asked.

"From a place called Birtwick. Thirty-two miles away," said James.

"Phew!" Towler whistled through his teeth. "That's quite a clip you set. I know a lot of coachmen – old chaps – couldn't cover half that distance with a pair of horses and a carriage that size."

"Really?" James squared his shoulders and smiled with pride. "It was up and down hill most of the way."

"Impressive!" Towler leant against the wheel of the carriage and puffed on his horrible pipe.

"You could start a fire with that thing – look at all this hay and straw," I said. Mr Manly would never have stood for anyone smoking in a stable yard.

"Don't you worry your little head, lad. I was looking after horses when you were a twinkle in your mother's eye." Towler laughed and tousled my spiky hair as if I was six years old. I saw him smirk at James over my head, as though they were both grown-ups together.

146

"James," I said, "tell him he shouldn't smoke."

"Oh leave it, Joe. Do," said James. He was leaning against the side of the carriage now too, chewing on a piece of straw like a farm boy at a harvest supper.

"Thing is," he explained, unbuttoning his livery coat and throwing it over his shoulder, "I had to put the drag on at least seven times in the last three miles ... without it the carriage would have been in the ditch."

I had no idea what a "drag" was, but James seemed very pleased with himself.

"Phew!" Towler whistled again. "That's where the skill is, see. You wouldn't believe the number of coachmen who come a cropper on that last bend."

"By the sawmill? Pah. That was nothing." I had never seen James like this before. Boasting and showing off. Being a coachman for the day had gone to his head. "You should see some of the tight bends we have back home," he said. "There's one, as you come towards Birtwick from the Beacon Hills..."

On and on they went about this turn, that turn – it was boring. I rolled my eyes and unbuckled Beauty's traces.

"Come on!" I slipped him out of the shafts. "Let's find you a stall."

I don't think either of the boys even noticed as I led him away. I found two empty stalls, far away from the other horses, right at the back of the stables.

"Nice and quiet for you, Beauty," I said as I went and fetched Ginger too.

I tied Ginger in the stall next to Beauty, then took off my smart green jacket and hung it on a nail on the wall. "We don't need their help, do we?" I said as I rolled my shirtsleeves up and rubbed both horses down with a cloth, especially where the harness had made them sweat.

Beauty scratched his head against me to get rid of the itch from his bridle.

"I am not a fence post!" I laughed as I nearly toppled over backwards. Even Ginger let me rub behind her ears. She really was a lovely mare once you got to know her.

As I ducked out of the stall, I saw that James had finally appeared.

"Finished showing off?" I said coolly.

"There's no need for that. I was only being friendly," he snapped. "Nice chap, that Dick Towler.

And from what he says he's had a lot of experience with horses. Beauty and Ginger are in safe hands."

"If you say so." I shrugged. I didn't really care whether Towler was friendly or not. I just didn't like the careless way he wandered around the stable with a burning pipe. James would normally have been the first to tell him off.

I climbed up into the hay loft above the horses' stalls and filled a good net for each of them.

When they were settled and fed at last, James and I went round to a servants' hall behind the kitchen for a bowl of stew.

We ate in silence, occasionally glaring at each other. Then we checked the horses once more before going up to our beds in an attic above the hotel.

I lay awake for a long time, listening to the sounds of the street outside. It was strange to be in a town with people talking and carts and carriages rattling past below. But it wasn't the noise that was keeping me awake. . .

"James," I whispered. It was dark in the attic but I sensed somehow that he was lying awake listening too. "Isn't it odd that we can't hear the horses?"

I had grown so used to sleeping right above them

in the loft. I always knew they were safe and well as long as I could hear the reassuring scrape of their hooves on the stones and the rustle as they moved in the straw.

"Just go to sleep, Joe," he snapped.

But I didn't, not for a long time.

Chapter Twenty-two

I must have fallen asleep at last. But I woke suddenly in the middle of the night and sat up with a start. There was an orange glow through the attic window – like a sunset, but it was still dark outside. There was the bitter smell of smoke in the air and sharp crackling sounds like a coachman cracking his whip.

"Fire!"

I don't know who shouted it first, me or James, but I know we were both on our feet in a moment.

Still in our nightshirts and long johns, we stamped our feet into our boots and thundered down the stairs to the yard.

"It's the stables!" I cried.

The ostler was rushing in and out of the stalls leading horses behind him. I could see Towler too, untying the row of horses nearest the big door.

"Move, you brutes. Move!" he cried, slapping them on the rumps and waving his arms wildly in the air. This only made the horses more frightened, of course. While some bolted for the yard, others reared up and refused to move at all. Luckily some other stable hands were doing a better job of urging the horses out to safety.

"Beauty and Ginger!" I said, grabbing James's arm. "They are right at the very back of the stable. We have to get them out of there."

If only I hadn't chosen the stalls furthest away from the doors.

"Hurry!" We plunged into the burning building.

The smoke at the front of the stable was thin like a summer mist. But the deeper inside we went, the thicker it became.

Somewhere in the fume-filled darkness I heard a terrified whinny. It was Beauty calling for help.

"Don't worry, I'm coming." I tried to call to him, but as I opened my mouth, my nose and throat filled with thick smoke. I doubled over, coughing and spluttering as I gasped for breath.

"Here!" James pulled his nightshirt over his head. As he stood bare-chested, he ripped at the ragged cotton and tore the shirt in two. "Tie this around your face," he said, throwing half to me. He covered his own mouth and nose as if the ripped shirt was a highwayman's mask.

I did the same as we stumbled on. Sweat prickled my neck. Although I could breathe more easily now my face was covered, the heat grew stronger. I could see the flickering orange glow at the heart of the fire burning in the roof. It must have started in the hay loft and was spreading all through the stables.

We reached the horses at last, scrambling over a fallen beam which was charred and smoking but no longer aflame.

"Beauty!" I flung myself towards him.

"Steady!" James grabbed my arm. "Don't let them know we're frightened."

Ginger was throwing her head wildly in the air but he stretched out and stroked her neck.

"Good girl," he soothed her. "Shall we go for a little walk now?"

From the way he spoke, he might have been leading Ginger out to the meadow to graze.

Beauty was stamping his feet, arching his neck and straining at the rope that tied him.

"Come along then. Let's get you out of here," I said, trying not to let my voice shake as I fumbled to untie the knot. It was so smoky I couldn't see what I was doing but at last I backed him out of the stall.

"Ready?" I tugged on his halter and brave Beauty took a big step forward.

"Come on, Ginger!" I could hear James coaxing the chestnut mare to follow. Calm as he was, she was too afraid to move. All she would do was throw her head in the air, shivering from top to toe.

Beauty turned and whinnied. He seemed to be telling Ginger to follow but she wouldn't leave the stall.

"Come on! Keep walking, boy!" I urged. Beauty reared up. He would not move now either. Not if his stablemate would not follow.

"Please!" I begged, turning around and trying to drag him behind me, pulling the rope over my shoulder like a sailor hauling a boat. The smoke was getting thicker and the crackling sound of the fire was almost deafening.

Beauty dug his toes in, flaring his nostrils.

It was no good. My eyes stung. I could see the

orange flames, licking the top of the ladder in the opening to the loft.

The roof above us shuddered and groaned.

"The whole lot will come down on us any minute," I cried.

"Run, Joe!" James coughed.

"No!" I shook my head.

"Do as I say, Joe. I'm head stable lad!" It was the first time James had raised his voice. "Go!"

I shook my head again.

"Not unless we can all go," I wheezed. "Beauty won't leave Ginger. And I won't leave Beauty."

"Stubborn fool!" James turned his back furiously but he did not try to fight me any more. "Come on, Ginger," he coaxed. "Come on, Ginger-girl, we've got to get you out of here."

"If only she had the blinkers from her harness," I whispered, talking more to Beauty than to James. Both horses wore eye guards to stop them being frightened of things when they pulled the carriage. If Ginger had her blinkers on she wouldn't take so much notice of the flames flickering across the wall like snakes. The ceiling groaned again.

"James!" I gasped, struck by a sudden thought. It wouldn't matter if we didn't have real blinkers so long as we could cover Ginger's eyes and stop her being frightened. All we needed was some cloth to throw over her head. I had seen Mr Manly do the same thing with a nervous filly to lead her past the pigsty once.

Thud! A burning plank fell to the floor spitting sparks like fiery rain.

Ginger snorted. Beauty whinnied with fear.

For a moment I considered ripping my own nightshirt off – even if it meant showing I was a girl – nothing mattered now except the horses. Then, with a leap of joy, I saw my fancy green coat; brass buttons reflecting the flames, draped on the nail where I'd hung it while rubbing down the horses last night.

"Here! Put this over Ginger's head," I cried, tossing the coat to James. He understood immediately and covered her eyes.

Ginger leapt forward.

"Come on, Beauty. She's coming with us. You lead the way." I gave his halter a little tug. He took a small step and began to follow me through the smoke towards the door. I knew he would be brave enough to walk without his eyes covered, just so long as Ginger and James were right behind us.

But we had only taken a few paces when Beauty refused to move again. I tugged him towards the left of a burning pillar but he pulled to the right, pushing me with his nose. I tried to pull to the left again – the gap was wider that side of the pillar – but he pushed me the other way, more firmly this time so that I almost stumbled.

"All right, boy. We'll do what you want." I let him lead me to the right and Ginger and James followed.

Seconds later, there was a terrible crash to the left of us. A great long beam from the burning hayloft fell to the floor, smashing to the ground.

"You saved us, Beauty!" I spluttered. If we'd gone the way I wanted to, the burning beam would have fallen right on top of our heads.

Smoke billowed all around us, but I could see a patch of light in the distance at last.

"Not long now!" croaked James. I clung to Beauty as we stumbled on.

The noise was terrible. The old building quaked and moaned. The fire was crackling loudly, horses were whinnying from the safety of the yard and so many voices were shouting from out there that I couldn't hear Ginger's hooves behind us any more.

I glanced over my shoulder as we reached the door to the fresh air outside at last.

"James?" I couldn't see him in the darkness.

Beauty hollered.

Then there was a billow of thick grey smoke and James and Ginger appeared again at last.

We burst into the fresh air of the yard together. People dashed forward and tried to take the horses from us, but James and I stumbled on.

We didn't stop until we'd led Beauty and Ginger out in to the market square, well away from the burning stable.

"We did it, Joe. We saved them," panted James.

"And Beauty saved us all," I said, as we flung our arms around our horses' necks and breathed in great gasping breaths of cold night air.

Chapter Twenty-three

As James and I stood patting Ginger and Beauty in the crowded marketplace, we heard the sound of galloping hooves and rumbling wheels coming towards us.

"Stand back! It's the fire engine," cried the ostler.

"Shift yourselves! Move out of the way," bellowed Towler. He was brave and brash again now he knew nobody would ask him to go into the burning building to rescue a horse. They were all safely outside now, thank goodness, and nobody was hurt.

I pulled Beauty up on to the pavement as two big dun-coloured cobs thundered over the stones dragging the heavy fire engine behind them. Three firemen leapt down from the back of the cart and began to unwind a long leather hose like a snake.

There was no need for them to ask where the fire was. Great orange flames leapt into the sky from the stable roof.

"This is all your fault," I said to Towler. "You and your stupid pipe!"

"You can't prove that!" He spun around and glared at me. "You can't prove nothing, so shut your mouth!"

"Now you listen here, Dick Towler," said James. Someone had given him a blanket to throw round his bare shoulders. He stood beside me as tall and proud as a prince in a cloak. "You're right. We'll probably never know for sure what started the fire. But I hope you'll always have doubt in your mind. I hope that'll make you more careful for the rest of your life."

"Ha! Who are you two tupenny-ha'penny country lads to tell me what to do?" Towler turned on his heel; but, as he walked away, his shoulders were hunched and his head was hung low.

"He can shout all he wants, but he feels guilty. You can see it written all over him," said James.

"Good!" I folded my arms and watched Towler slink away into the crowd.

"He's not the only one to blame." James shifted his feet and stared at his boots. "I should have listened to you, Joe. You were right; no decent horseman would smoke around a stable. It was wrong from the start."

"No harm done," I said, but I felt my eyes fill up with tears of relief. It was over. Beauty and Ginger were safe. And James and I were friends again at last.

"We're quite a team, you and me," he said, stepping closer. For a minute I thought he was going to hug me. Then I remembered I was a boy and we slapped each other awkwardly on the back before we turned away and quickly patted the horses too. "Quite a team!" said James again.

"Just like Beauty and Ginger," I said, hiding behind the dear black horse as I wiped my sooty eyes.

When I looked up again, the squire was hurrying across the market square towards us. His face was lined with worry.

"Thank you, my boys!" He shook us both warmly by the hand. "I have never seen such bravery. You saved our beloved horses. The mistress was quite beside herself with fear for you all."

He patted both the horses and then turned and shook James's hand again.

"Manly will be very proud when he hears how you acted tonight. You'd be fit to be a coachman anywhere in the land."

"Thank you, sir!" James flushed with pride.

As the master turned to me, I beamed too.

"As for you," he said, staring down at me in the lamplight. "I have realized something tonight. You are not a boy..."

"Not ... not a boy?" My heart jumped suddenly into my mouth.

"You are not a boy," said the squire, laying his hands on my shoulder, "... because tonight, Joe, you became a man!"

"Oh! Thank you!" My words came out in a rush as I dared to breathe.

"You are both fine, brave young men," said Squire Gordon, shaking hands with me and James all over again. "And I thank you from the bottom of my heart."

After the terrible dramas of that night, it was decided that we should leave in the early hours of the morning. The mistress had been overcome by shock and the horses were still shaken.

"It is best if we return to Birtwick right away," said the master. "The mistress will visit her sister at another time."

He was in such a hurry to be gone that James and I had found no time to wash, except to rinse our hands and faces in a bucket of cold water.

"Just look at the state of me," sighed James, brushing ash from his hair.

"At least you still have your smart green coat." I smiled. Somebody had found him a shirt to wear too. But my green jacket had been lost in the all the commotion. The last time I saw it, it was covering Ginger's eyes.

I was afraid the mistress would be displeased to ride with a pair of such sooty and dishevelled servants. But she smiled as she climbed shakily into the carriage. "You both look like the fine brave boys you are. Coming home with two horses and our stable lads is far more important than any coat," she said.

Even so, James and I must have made a funny sight, sitting up on top of the grand carriage.

"We look like a couple of chimney sweeps," James said with a laugh.

I didn't mind. At least we had brushed the horses

a little. They seemed to know at once that we were heading home. None the worse for their night of adventure, they pricked their ears and trotted out along the lanes. James and I chatted like old friends again.

I thought how wonderful it would be to ride Ginger and Beauty across the common together. It would be autumn soon and we'd see the leaves in the highwood change from green to gold.

But, as we reached Birtwick village, the master banged his stick on the roof of the coach.

"Faster, please," he begged. "We must get home. The mistress is not well."

A week later, we heard that Birtwick Park was to be closed up.

"The family are going away," explained Mr Manly. He had taken me and James aside in the stables to break the sad news; his face was grim. "They are going to Italy. The mistress must have warmer weather for her health and the winters in England are bad for her. They will stay abroad indefinitely."

"But what about the horses?" I cried. "What about Merrylegs and Ginger?" My voice was shaking. "What about Beauty?" I was trying hard not to be selfish, but I couldn't help it; I had to know what would happen to us all.

"Merrylegs is to go to vicarage; Miss Jessie and Miss Flora are going to stay there with their governess until their mother is strong again," said Mr Manly. I could tell from his voice that he was sad too. "But all the other horses must be sold."

"Sold?" I felt numb. "But where will Beauty go?" After all the adventures we had shared, I cared about him more than anything else in the whole world.

"He'll go to whoever will pay a fair price for him," said Mr Manly. "And we must all find new work too." He glanced down the drive towards his cottage where his wife was standing by the garden gate, cradling their newborn son.

"It's not fair!" I cried. "We can't be sent away. We live here. This is our home."

"Not without the squire," said James. His face was pale and his mouth was set in a hard line. "Servants and horses cannot stay in a house without a mistress or a master. The squire will do his best for us but—"

"No!" I couldn't listen to another word. I ran towards the stables. There had to be some way to stop this. I wasn't a servant. Not really. I was the daughter of Sir Charles Green ... or I was once. There had to be something I could do.

As Beauty saw me charging towards him, he lifted his head and whinnied over the loose-box door.

I flung my arms around his neck.

"Oh, Beauty," I cried. "What are we going to do?"

Chapter
Twenty-four

Miss Jessie and Miss Flora were the first to leave the big house. They moved into the vicarage with their governess. Although confused by all the upheaval, they seemed happy enough to stay with the vicar and his young family, at least until their mother was settled overseas.

I led Merrylegs up the road to join them the next day. "You be a good boy now, won't you?" I said, kissing his nose as I let him into the little paddock beside the church.

"Don't worry, Joe. I'll look after him," promised Flora, swinging on the gate.

"I know you will," I said.

I wished I could tell her how Merrylegs had

once been my pony and how jealous I had been when she first rode him. But I knew now that what made Merrylegs truly happy was having someone young to pet and ride him ... and bring him plenty of apples, carrots and sugar lumps, of course.

"Goodbye, old friend," I whispered in his soft ears, as Flora climbed down from the gate and began to rummage through her pockets looking for a treat. At least amidst all the uncertainty I knew Merrylegs was safe; the kindly vicar had promised he could live out his days in the paddock even if Jessie and Flora moved abroad to join their parents later.

Flora flung her arms around my waist.

"I wish you didn't have to go away, Joe," she whispered.

"Me too, Miss Flora," I said. "Me too."

If only we could all have stayed at Birtwick: Flora and Merrylegs. James and Ginger. Me and Beauty...

But it wasn't to be. Our whole world was about to be torn apart.

The squire did all he could to find kind homes for the horses and jobs for the staff.

The twins were to work in the gardens of a big estate near to their mother.

"It is all very well, but I hoped we would be off to London for a real adventure, like Dick Whittington," said Wilf with a sigh.

"I'm just glad we'll be able to pop home for a slice of Mother's apple pie on Sundays," said Sid.

Caleb was to be apprenticed as a butcher's boy in the village, something which seemed to fill him with joy.

"I can already skin a rabbit in seven seconds," he beamed.

Daisy was to be housemaid for the doctor. And Doris had found a job in the White Lion hotel, where we had stayed on the night of the fire.

Mr Manly was to go all the way to Devonshire, where one of the squire's oldest friends ran a stud.

"Mrs M is quite beside herself with excitement," he chuckled. "Our new cottage has a view of the sea. And Squire Gordon has given us old Justice and the cart to keep for ourselves."

Several of the other horses were going to the Devonshire stud too but the master there had no need for Ginger or Beauty. He had no need for any new stable lads either. So James and I had nowhere to go. Every day we hoped for news – that work might have been found for us – but every day there was nothing. James grew more and more worried.

"I don't care where we go," I whispered to Black Beauty. "We'll live wild like gypsies on the road, just so long as we can be together."

Finally, the morning arrived of the master and mistress's departure, and James and I still had no idea of our fate.

We had harnessed Ginger and Beauty to the coach so we could take the master and mistress to the station. The squire came down the steps from the big house carrying Mrs Gordon in his arms. She had her eyes half closed and looked pale and worn.

James held the horses' heads while I opened the carriage door.

"Ah. Little Joe," the mistress murmured, lifting her head with an effort. "You were such a favourite with our Flora. And I have good news – I have found a place for you. . ."

The squire laid the mistress gently down on the cushions inside the carriage.

"Save your breath, my dear. Allow me to explain," he said.

He gestured for me to follow him towards James and the horses.

"My poor wife was so very anxious to find you both a position," he said. "As was I, of course. She has been writing notes for days, even though the doctor told her she must not vex herself. And then, last night, at last, an answer came. It is from Earlshall Park where the Earl of Westop lives. The countess is looking for a new pageboy to ride on her carriage and my wife told her how splendid you looked in your livery, Joe."

"That is very kind, sir." I tried my best to sound pleased. I was about to open my mouth and ask what would happen to Beauty when the squire carried on.

"Better still, Mr York, the coachman there, is looking for a new under-groom. It will be a promotion for you, James, but I have sent word that I cannot think of a better man for the job."

"Thank you, sir." James bowed his head, but he did not look as happy as I might have expected. Every stable lad dreamed of becoming a groom. Perhaps James was like me, and all he could think about was Ginger. He loved that difficult old mare almost as much I loved Beauty, I think.

"Well, then," the squire said, with a contented nod. "Let's begin the journey, shall we?"

"Wait! If you please, sir," I caught hold of his sleeve; James shot me an iron look, but I did not let go. "What is to happen to the horses?"

"These two?" Squire Gordon stroked Ginger and Beauty's forelocks. "Did I not say? They are coming with you to live at Earlshall Park. You are to drive the carriage over there later today."

"Oh thank you, sir!" I flung my arms around the squire's neck, even though I heard James gasp with shock. "Thank you, mistress." I dashed to the carriage, stuck my head through the open doorway and blew her a kiss.

"You are very welcome, Joe." She smiled and tried to lift her head.

"Right. Well, yes. Best be off." The squire looked so surprised that anyone would think I had thrown a bucket of water over his head.

"Joe!" James hissed at me. I paid no attention. I ducked under his arm, kissed Ginger's nose and buried my head in Beauty's mane.

"Everything is going to be all right now. We will be together," I said.

*

I thought Beauty might be scared when we reached the railway station. The steam train was puffing and billowing like a dragon. I should have known better. Although Ginger fretted and squirmed, Beauty stood still as a statue, flicking his ears to show he was interested but not afraid.

"Brave boy!" I held the horses' heads, while James – who was stronger and taller – helped the squire carry the mistress to the platform.

"Goodbye, boys. God bless you," she called.

"Good luck," said the master.

"Thank you! Goodbye," James called out. But I could not speak. It was all too much; my joy and relief knowing I would be with Beauty after all, and my worry wondering if the poor mistress would ever see her little girls or return to England again.

I slipped behind the Beauty to hide my tears.

Then the guard whistled and the train rattled away.

James watched till it was out of sight, then rejoined me at the carriage.

"We will never see that poor lady again," he said quietly. "Never."

"She was our guardian angel," I said. It was true. She would never know how grateful I was for her kindness, or that even at the very end she had always thought of others, and found a way for Beauty and I to stay together.

"Goodbye," I whispered, although she was long gone. Then I climbed up beside James on the carriage as he turned the horses around, ready to head for Earlshall Park, our new home.

Part Three
Earlshall Park

Chapter Twenty-five

As we trotted along the country roads, I was so pleased to be with Beauty that I wanted to sing. But I was afraid my high singing voice – so different from the gruff mumblings I used as Joe the groom – would give me away for sure. Instead I whistled a happy tune – it was something I had got very good at since pretending to be a boy. I glanced over at James, hoping he'd join in, but I saw he was biting his lip and looking as grey as the clouds that had gathered above our heads.

"Are you all right?" I asked. "Aren't you pleased to have a new job? It's a promotion. And with Ginger and Beauty too?"

"Of course I'm pleased." James stared straight ahead.

"If you're nervous about being an under-groom, don't be," I said. "Mr Manly always said you'd be a coachman before you were twenty and. . ."

"No. It's not that. I know I can do a good job with the horses," said James.

"Then what?"

"I've just heard things, that's all." James shrugged. "About the kind of stable they run at Earlshall Park. And the mistress. She likes things done very differently than we're used to at Birtwick."

"Well," I said brightly. "Change can be a good thing."

I should know, I thought as I began to whistle again. I'd had more changes than an actor on the stage in the last six months. And it has all turned out much better than I could ever have hoped. There was no reason to think this next adventure should be any different.

It was afternoon when we finally arrived at Earlshall. Ginger shied as we turned through a gate with big stone dogs snarling down at us.

"Steady," said James, but she was still spooked and Beauty laid his ears flat.

A dim drizzle started as we trotted up the

sweeping drive. It was the sort of thin, steady rain that washed all the colour out of the world and got right down inside the neck of my shirt. Even Beauty's shiny black coat looked sooty and dull and Ginger's bright chestnut fur seemed muddy-brown.

I hunched my shoulders and wiped the rain from my eyes as the buildings came into view. Earlshall Park was so huge it made Birtwick look like a dolls' house. It was four times bigger than even Summer's Place. But there was nothing pretty about it. It was grey and square like a fortress with big stone pillars at the front.

We were about to turn the carriage down the side of the house towards the stable block, when the huge front door was flung open by a footman wearing white stockings and scarlet breeches.

"Halt!" he cried. "Lady Westop wishes to examine the new horses."

"Right you are." James drew us to a halt and I jumped down from the top of the carriage to hold the horses' heads.

The footman stood on the steps in the rain. He carried a rolled-up umbrella but it was clearly for the countess and soon his well-oiled black hair had begun to drip. James was dripping too, perched on top of the carriage. I could hide between Ginger and Beauty a little, but as the drizzle turned to rain, I was soon sopping wet as well.

I glanced at the stable clock. It was two o'clock in the afternoon.

Beauty and Ginger hung their heads and shivered. Still we waited.

Half past two. I couldn't stand it any longer.

"Excuse me!" I called across to the footman. "Do you think Lady Westop has changed her mind? Shall we take the horses to the stables and get them dry?"

"Shh!" James and the footman both hushed me at once.

"What?" I whispered at James. "It's pointless us just standing here if she's not coming."

"She will come," said the footman, staring straight ahead and not even blinking although rain was running down his face.

"When?" I groaned.

"When she is ready." The footman sneezed.

The poor man was getting a chill. But I could tell it was hopeless. Nobody would dare to move until Lady Westop finally came out. Even if that was tomorrow morning. . .

I tried not to watch the hands on the clock.

Three... Quarter past three... The rain stopped but we were damp and chilly. It wasn't summer any more and the late September wind was cold.

Ginger was jostling and fretting with her bit. Beauty had gone to sleep, I think. His head was resting on my shoulder.

At four o'clock it began to rain again.

Half past four. Two and a half hours we had been standing there. All of us – the footman, James and I, and the horses – were silent with exhaustion.

The door swung open.

There was a rustling sound of silk. A tall thin woman with a nose like a bird's beak appeared on the top of the steps. Her dress was white and she was wearing a black ostrich feather hat. It made her look like a magpie.

"One for sorrow," I whispered under my breath, remembering how Nanny Clay always touched her head if she saw one of the black-and-white birds on its own, saying it was a sign of bad luck.

The footman dashed forward, raising the umbrella even though it had stopped raining again now and there was even a little late afternoon sun.

"These are the horses?" Lady Westop was still

standing on the steps. I had no idea if she was talking to me or the footman or James.

"Yes, my lady." We all answered at once.

"There is no need to shout!" she snapped.

Still not leaving the steps, she lifted a little pair of eye-glasses on a gold chain around her neck and peered through them.

"But they do not match!"

Nobody answered her for a moment.

"I say, they do not match!" she repeated. "One horse is chestnut and one is black."

James cleared his throat.

"They are both fifteen and a half hands high and very well suited to each other in the carriage," he said. "They are forward-going with a lovely rhythm. Squire Gordon always said. . ."

"Enough!" cried Lady Magpie (as I had decided to call her). "I have no need to hear the views of a shabby country squire communicated to me by a stable boy who looks like a drowned rat." She held up her hand. James shrivelled into silence.

"These horses are a different colour!" she said, as if the rest of us were blind. "It will not do." Then she turned back into the house. The footman scuttled after her and the door closed behind them.

"That's it?" I said, as James climbed down from the carriage. "We have waited for hours in the rain just to be told that Ginger is chestnut and Beauty is black?"

"What she means is that they are not fashionable," explained James despondently. "All the really smart carriages are pulled by two bays or two chestnuts or two black horses – a perfect matching pair."

"She barely even looked at them. She didn't even say how beautiful they are!" I cried.

I patted both horses as we led the carriage round to the stable yard at last.

"Don't you listen to that sour old magpie," I whispered in Beauty's ear. "You and Ginger are perfect."

Earshall's head groom stepped out of his office as we pulled into the stable yard.

"James Howard?" he said.

"Pleased to meet you, Mr York. And this is Joe Green," said James. "We are very grateful to you for taking us both on. And these are the two new horses from Birtwick."

"Fine beasts. Especially the black one." Mr York looked inside Ginger and Beauty's mouths. "What did Her Ladyship make of them?"

"She said they do not match," reported James.

"Ah!" Mr York nodded. "She will not like them harnessed like this either. She will want them in bearing reins."

"Bearing reins?" A look of panic flashed into James's eyes. "Squire Gordon did not approve of bearing reins, sir. We believe Ginger might have been forced to use them before, but never Beauty."

"What are bearing reins?" I asked.

"They force the horse to hold its head up high," explained James. "But it means they put a terrible strain on the horses' backs and necks when they pull a carriage up hill."

"It is the fashion," said Mr York crisply. "Her Ladyship insists on the very tightest rein." He shrugged. "You shouldn't even be round here, lad. Get up to the house and let us settle the horses."

He began to shoo me away.

"What do you mean? Am I not to work in the stables too?" I said.

"Lady Westop does not like her pageboys to get dirty. You will only be needed when the carriage is going out for a drive and then you will be sent for," said Mr York.

"But ... please, let me help with the horses," I

begged. "I'll sleep in a stall with Black Beauty if there isn't room for me anywhere else. I don't mind. I'd like that."

"You will sleep in the house," said Mr York firmly.

"Joe really is a wonderful stable lad," said James.

Beauty turned his head towards me, sensing my panic.

But it was no good. Mr York had begun to unharness him.

"I am sorry. You are a pageboy now," he said. "Lady Westop has her rules and she must be obeyed."

Chapter
Twenty-six

I was shown to a small airless room, no bigger than a coffin, in the servants' wing. There was no draught and no spiders like there had been in the loft at Birtwick, but there was no window either, except for a tiny slit like the slash of a whip, too high up to look out of.

I missed the sound of the horses and the chatter of the twins – even if Wilf's feet did smell like rotten cheese. I wondered how they were getting on. Little Flora too. I thought of the mistress and master, all that long way away in a foreign land. Most of all, I thought about James and Ginger and Beauty and how they were settling into the stables. I wished I could be down there with them.

At least I'm here, I told myself, as I tossed and turned all night. *At least I am close to Beauty.*

The next morning I dressed myself in the white tights and red breeches that had been laid out for me, as well as a frilly white shirt and a scarlet jacket with twelve gold buttons. I felt like a toy soldier.

"What should I do?" I asked the butler, a stiff cold-eyed man called Mr Graves, when I had finished my breakfast. The other servants bustled around me with brushes and buckets and mops. "Where should I go until the carriage is needed?"

"Follow me," said Mr Graves, hurrying upstairs with a note on a silver tray. He stopped in the grand entrance hall. Two footmen stood silently on either side of the big front door.

"Stand there." The butler pointed to a spot on the black and white magpie-coloured tiles. "Do not fidget and do not step outside the square." He tapped one white tile with his foot. "When the carriage comes to the front of the house, you must go outside and sit up on the box seat, nice and still."

"That's it?" I gasped. "I have to stand here all day?

And then I sit on the carriage like an ornament on a shelf?"

"Yes. That's it," said Mr Graves. And he was gone.

The two footmen stood as still as statues staring straight ahead. I tried to pass the time by counting the black and white tiles. Three hundred and seventy two. Then I tried to remember the dates of all the kings and queens of England and all of Henry the Eighth's six wives – although I think I got Jane Seymour and Anne of Cleves the wrong way round. Then I closed my eyes and imagined I was riding Beauty. We were galloping across the common at Birtwick, then trotting past the watermill . . . just for fun, we leapt the stream.

"Psst!" The footman was hissing at me. "It's forbidden to fall asleep," he whispered.

"I'm not," I said. "I'm just closing my eyes."

"Shh!" The other footman wagged his finger. "No closing your eyes."

So that was it, I had to stand there with my eyes wide open, staring straight ahead. The worst of it was, there was a grandfather clock right in front of me that chimed every quarter of an hour.

"Do you think the mistress will call for the carriage soon?" I whispered at eleven o'clock.

"No chance." The first footman shook his head. "Her Ladyship does not get out of bed until noon."

"Then why have I been standing here since eight o'clock this morning?" I asked.

"Shhh!" The footmen hissed at me in unison like geese.

We were each given twenty minutes break for lunch. First one footman, then the other. Then me.

Then it was back to standing still as the afternoon ticked slowly by. How I longed for a horse to brush or a harness to scrub. I would have mucked out twenty stables rather than stand there another minute.

At last, at quarter to three, I heard the sound of horses' hooves outside and another footman appeared in the hall.

"The carriage is summoned," he said.

I leapt forward, flung open the door even before the footmen could get there and bolted down the steps.

Beauty whinnied with delight. He tried to lift his neck to look round at me. But something was stopping him. A thick leather strap ran from the ring of his bit, up along the side of his head and was clipped tight to the harness on his back.

"A bearing rein," I said in horror. "He can't even look at me properly."

"I know," James said with a sigh. "I have fastened them as loose as I dare."

Ginger was fretting terribly, rolling her eyes and stamping her feet.

"Poor things, it must be worse than a whalebone corset," I cried.

"Quick!" James sat up straight and I dashed to the side of the carriage as the front door opened behind me.

The countess rustled down the steps.

"You," she said clicking her fingers at James. "Peter..."

"Apologies... It's, er, James ... James Howard, madam," he said, climbing down from the top of the carriage.

"Nonsense. The last boy was Peter and I shall call you Peter. I have no time to learn new names."

"As you wish." James bowed his head, but not before I saw his grey eyes flash.

I think Lady Magpie saw it too. She smiled with satisfaction as if she had scored a point in a game of cards.

She did not ask my name or even look in my direction.

"Peter, you must put these horses' heads higher," she said to James. "They are not fit to be seen."

"I beg your pardon, My Lady," said James very respectfully. "But these horses have never been reined up before. If the bearing rein must be used at all, I think it would be better to introduce it slowly. That way, at least, the horses can get used to it."

"You think so, do you, Peter?" Lady Magpie glared at him with her beady little eyes.

"Yes, Your Ladyship." James did not flinch. "I do think it would be best."

"Well nobody asked you to think, did they, Peter? Your job is to drive my horses in whatever way I see fit," Lady Magpie snapped. "Kindly tighten those reins right away. At least three holes. I wish to visit my sister-in-law at Eastleigh and her horses are always reined high."

Biting his lip, James went round to Beauty's head and began to fiddle with the strap. I stepped back as the two footmen rushed forward to open the carriage door and help Lady Magpie inside.

"It is bad enough the horses do not match," she continued as she climbed in. "The very least I can ask is that they be presented with some sense of style."

"As you wish, Your Ladyship," said James through

gritted teeth. I watched as he pulled the reins a little tighter, but by only one hole.

I stepped forward so that Beauty could see me out of the corner of his eye. He would know I was here at least. He rolled his eyes and looked at me imploringly but there was nothing I could do. I wasn't even a stable boy anymore – I was a toy solider in a stupid costume.

The footmen stood on the back of the carriage and then James and I climbed up to the box seat on top. I had no job at all except to sit in my scarlet suit. When we had worn our livery to drive to the White Lion with Squire Gordon and the mistress it had seemed like dressing up for a bit of fun. But this was a terrible sort of showing off on a much grander scale. We were only going five miles down the country roads.

Unfortunately, four of those five miles were uphill.

Poor Beauty. Poor Ginger. Now I began to understand how truly terrible the bearing reins were. Instead of stretching their heads forward to help pull the weight of the heavy carriage up the steep slopes, they were forced to keep their heads up high and pull with all the strain on their backs.

It would be like me carrying a load of bricks with my arms held straight in the air above my shoulders, never being allowed to bend my elbows to help take the strain.

"It'll be bad coming back downhill too," whispered James. "The horses can't see their feet."

Each day was the same. I would stand silently in the hall for hours and then, usually some time around three, the carriage would be summoned.

Each day, Lady Magpie would demand the bearing reins were tightened as far as they would go. James would always silently disobey, tightening the reins by just one hole. Even so, poor Ginger laid her ears flat against her head and kicked and wriggled in the shafts. Her mouth frothed and she stumbled terribly – twice falling on her knees so that James and I had to jump down from the carriage and help her up again.

Beauty stayed calm and dignified, never showing how much strain the reins must have put on him. But even he could not hide the way his neck quivered and his poor mouth frothed as the terrible tight bit jabbed him.

"I can't stand this, James," I whispered as we heaved up the hill again for the fifth time that week.

Lady Magpie had finally had her way that morning, and the horses' heads were pulled up as high as they would go.

"Don't worry, Joe." James forced himself to smile. "At least it can't get any worse. There are no more holes in the bearing reins."

But James was wrong.

"Higher, Peter!" cried Lady Magpie the next day, as she approached the carriage. "Are you never going to get those horses' heads up as I ask?"

"They are as high as they can go, My Lady," said James gently. "The reins have no more holes."

"Then you must call York," she ordered. "We will just have to make more holes."

James did not move. His face was dark and mutinous. There was a horrible pause and then Lady Magpie gave a cruel little smile.

"York! Where are you?" she called, shouting towards the stable. "Bring a leather punch, right away."

"No!" I gasped. I couldn't bear it a moment longer. I dashed forward, flinging myself between her and Beauty. "Stop it!" I cried, ignoring the look of astonishment on her beaky face. "Just leave those poor horses alone!"

Chapter
Twenty-seven

"What did you say?" Lady Magpie glared at me. She was almost quivering with fury.

"I said, leave those poor horses alone. It is terrible to pull their heads up so high." My legs were trembling. But nothing could have stopped me now. Not even James, whose eyes were pleading with me to be quiet.

"It's stupid and cruel, Lady Westop," I snapped. "If you're so keen to look smart, then tie your own head up with a rein. See how that feels."

Thwack.

She swooped so fast I did not see it coming. She had grabbed the long coachman's whip from the side of the carriage and lashed it against my face.

"How dare you speak to me like that," she cried as I fell to the ground. "You are nothing, do you hear me? Nothing. Not even the dirt on my shoe."

All the time she was talking, she was still beating me, bringing the lash of the whip sharply down. It stung my arms and shoulders, ripping through the thin tights on my legs as I curled into a ball and buried my face.

"Please, My Lady!" From the corner of my eye I could see James grasping her arm. "Please stop!"

I saw Beauty rear up. His ears were laid flat against his head and he was turning his neck and trying desperately to bite her. But he could not reach. He wanted to protect me but the bearing rein was too tight.

Thwack!

The whip stung my cheek like a hornet.

"Please." James was talking to her soothingly, as he would a difficult horse, but I could hear a note of terror in his voice. "You must stop."

And as suddenly as she had begun, she did stop, tossing the whip down on top of me. "I am ready to go for my drive now," she said, turning to James as if nothing at all had happened. She lifted her skirts and stepped over me to get to the carriage.

"You," she said, glaring down at me from her seat,

"you will go to the servants' quarters, fetch your things and leave. By the time I return, it will be as if you were never here."

"No. . . Don't send me away. Please." I sat up, my face and shoulders throbbing. Blood trickled down my cheek from my ear. I had to stay at Earlshall, I had to be with Beauty.

"My Lady – please reconsider," said James. "There is nowhere for Joe to go, not without references. Could you do that for him at least?"

"He can rot in the workhouse for all I care." She drew herself up and eyed him haughtily. "And if you say another word, you will be joining him."

James opened his mouth but I caught his eye and lifted a shaky finger to my lips. There was no point in us both losing our jobs, not when Beauty and Ginger would need us more than ever. How could I have been so stupid? I felt sick to my stomach.

"Leave those smart livery clothes; I do not want you taking them," said Lady Magpie, looking down at me one last time. "I should have known better than to hire a redhead. You may be a pretty little thing, boy, but you have a temper like the devil."

"Please, My Lady." I scrambled to my feet. "I will never be rude to you again—"

"Silence!" she snapped, and she slammed the door of the carriage before the startled footman could even move to assist her.

"You fool, Joe. You've been no help to Beauty. Not like this." James's face was pale and a muscle in his cheek was pumping as he picked up the whip from the ground and climbed into the driving seat. "Walk on!" he said loudly.

But, although Ginger took a step, Beauty would not move. He would not leave me. He scraped his hoof furiously on the ground and tried to turn his head.

"Walk on," said James again. Then he lifted the whip, something I had never seen him do.

"Go, Beauty!" I cried. "Go on!"

Then I stumbled away around the side of the house. Anything rather than see Beauty hurt any more than he already had been. Especially not because of me.

I washed my face in the water trough until the stinging in my cheek stopped. But I felt numb all over.

Even when Mr York shouted and told me I was an insolent young fool, I couldn't really think about what I had done.

I went upstairs to my narrow room, took off the scarlet livery and got dressed again in my own simple, ragged clothes. Billy's clothes. Joe Green's clothes – the boy I had worked so hard to become. Was that all over now? Had I thrown it all away? Where would I go? What would I do? My mind was whirring. But I knew one thing; Beauty and I would not be separated. I would find a way.

As I was turning to leave the tiny room, the bright red livery caught my eye. I had laid it on the bed; the scarlet pageboy's jacket, the bright red breeches and the white tights – ripped in places by the whip. . . The whole ridiculous solider suit.

Lady Magpie had been so firm that I should leave it behind.

"She can have the stupid thing," I muttered. "She's welcome to it!"

But as I went to close the door behind me, I stopped.

I dug inside the small cloth bag where I kept my few belongings – a comb, a clean handkerchief, Flora's book of fairy tales that she had insisted I keep. And the pair of big sharp scissors I carried everywhere to make sure I kept my hair cropped short.

Snip! Snip! Snip!

The tights fell first like snow.

I kept on cutting.

In a matter of moments, the breeches and jacket were nothing more than tattered shreds littering the floor.

My hands were still shaking as I stared down at the mess. There was no turning back. No apology I could make. Nanny Clay had always said my temper would get me into trouble. Now it had.

Strangely, although I was trembling, I felt very calm inside. Calm and clear-headed.

The only person whose temper was worse than mine was Lady Magpie. With all her cruel fury, she had set me free from Earlshall Park.

I would not leave here without Beauty. I would set him free too.

Chapter
Twenty-eight

"Stop!"

It was the middle of the night and I had been hiding in the fields waiting for this moment all day. But I had barely slipped Beauty's bridle over his head when James stepped out of the shadows.

"You little fool," he whispered. "I knew that you would do something like this. I knew you would try to steal Black Beauty."

"And I shall." I glared at him, my fingers still working on the buckles of Beauty's bridle. "How can you even think I would leave him here? If you had any sense, you'd come too."

Suddenly my heart was thudding faster. Not with fear but with excitement.

"That's it! We'll all go . . . you, me, Beauty, Ginger. All four of us. We can be together," I cried.

James leant back against the manger and didn't speak for a minute. When he did, his voice was low. "You haven't been telling the truth, have you?" he said. "You're not who you say you are, Joe Green."

He looked me up and down in the darkness of the stable. I felt a sudden rush of relief. So he had guessed my secret at last. It didn't matter now anyway. Not if I was going to take Beauty and run away.

"James," I said. "I. . ."

"There's no need for you to say anything," James interrupted, still keeping his voice low. "I can see it as clear as the nose on my face. You're not a working boy, Joe. I don't know what it is you're hiding. But you've never been poor in your life."

So that's what he had guessed; not that I was a girl but that I had once been rich.

"I can hear it in the way you talk. I can see it in the way you stand," he said. "You have so much pride, Joe. It's like you think you are better than everyone else."

"No, I don't. I don't think I am better than you,

James." There wasn't a bone in my body that thought that. "You taught me everything. How to care for horses. How to be a stable boy."

"No real stable boy would answer that old magpie back like you did today," said James. "It's like you think you're her equal."

"I'm not her equal," I said. "I'm better than her! Much better. And so are you!"

"In God's eyes, maybe." James shrugged. "But it's the likes of Lady Magpie who rule this world. Even good masters like Squire Gordon. They decide whether I eat or not. Whether I have somewhere safe to sleep. It's people like them, Joe. People like you..."

I didn't know what to say. How to begin to explain. If only he'd steal Ginger and run away with me – I could take my time, I could tell him everything. But I knew that he never would.

I stroked Beauty's head as he nuzzled against me. "You won't come, will you, James?" I said.

"I can't." James sighed. "You can never understand, Joe. You've never had to wake up hungry and go to bed again with no food in your belly that night."

"Yes I have," I said. "Twice." The day I'd escaped from Aunt Lavinia in the hay cart and again when Daisy and Doris dressed me in Miss Jessie's nightdress and I was banished to the loft.

"Twice?" James laughed. "I am talking about every day. My father had nothing, just a skinny horse and a broken-down cart. He was a rag-and-bone man, until he couldn't pay the grain merchant and had to sell the horse. That was the end of him. Bronchitis. Took him within a month. My mother too."

"I didn't know," I said. "I'm so sorry."

"Don't be." James's jaw was set hard. "I was lucky. Squire Gordon took me on as a stable lad. But I'm not like you, Joe. Leaving a paid job isn't a choice for me. In a year or two I hope I can look for a position as head groom somewhere. Until then, I'm stuck here. Being good. Being careful."

"Fine," I said. "But you won't stand in my way, will you? You won't stop me taking Beauty?"

"I certainly will stop you." James stood up.

"Just to save yourself and your precious job?" I cried.

"Hush! Do you want to bring the whole house running?" James put his finger to his lips. "It's to save *you*, Joe. Horse theft is a serious crime. It doesn't matter who you are – they'll throw you in prison. It's not that long ago they would have hanged you by the neck."

"They won't catch me," I said. "You know how fast Beauty gallops. We'll hide in the woods. We'll roam the open roads like gypsies." My words sounded hollow even to me. It was beginning to sound like the sort of thing Nanny Clay would have rolled her eyes at. A silly, childish dream.

"They'll find you in hours," whispered James. "Days at most. Black Beauty is a special horse. Everyone will notice when you ride into a town to buy corn. Every blacksmith in every tiny village for three counties will have heard his description by tomorrow afternoon. What'll you do when he needs new shoes?"

"I don't know," I said desperately. "But I've got to try."

"And get yourself arrested? How will that help Beauty?"

"Stop!" I felt as if I had been thumped in the stomach by a charging bull. But I knew James was right.

"Then … then I'll leave Beauty here in the stables," I said, desperately. "But I'll hide in the fields nearby. I'll live on berries and fruit. There's

205

an old shepherd's hut by the bridge. The roof has fallen in but it will give me some shelter. I'll watch Beauty go past in the carriage. I'll creep up here at night. I am not going away without him, James. I can't."

"All very well while there are blackberries in the hedges and the weather holds," said James. "But what about next month when the leaves fall off the trees? Or December and January when the snow comes? What'll you do then?"

"I'll be all right," I said. "I'll survive."

James sighed. "You won't. You're soft, Joe. You'll freeze to death. And what good will that do for your precious horse?"

"I don't know," I wailed.

"Go to Riverford," said James. "It's about ten miles from here as the crow flies."

"Or as the magpie squawks," I mumbled, trying to smile.

James ignored me.

"The White Lion have rebuilt their stables after the fire," he said. "A coaching inn like that is always on the lookout for help – anyone who is handy with the horses – especially if you're prepared to work cheap in exchange for food and lodgings. Doris from Birtwick has a job there already. You know, the pretty one with dark hair? Daisy's friend."

"She's not that pretty," I said quickly.

James carried on. "Perhaps if you're nice, she'll vouch for you."

"What about Beauty?" I said.

"I'll look after him. I give you my solemn promise," said James. "I'll even try to persuade Lady Magpie to loosen the bearing reins."

"I wouldn't worry about that." I smiled weakly and showed him my scissors. "I went into the tack room and cut all the bearing reins into pieces."

"Joe, you didn't!" James looked shocked but he was smiling.

It was chopping up the silly red suit that gave me the idea.

"Lady Magpie always sends her maids into Riverford in the dog cart to buy buttons and lace," said James. "And the groom drives them. I'll make sure it's me and Beauty who come, and that way you can get to see him."

"Maybe," I said slowly. It wasn't perfect but at least I'd get to be with Beauty sometimes. That had to be better than nothing.

"The earl goes to Riverford whenever there's a

horse fair too," said James. "He always takes a groom in case he buys anything and needs it ridden back."

"You'll find me every time? And you'll keep Beauty safe, James – you promise?"

"I will," he said. Then he leant into the manger and pulled out a hunk of bread and cheese which he must have hidden away, sure that I'd come into the stables to try and take Beauty tonight. "Good luck, Joe."

"You too," I whispered. "And thank you. I'll see you soon."

Then James slipped out of the stable, leaving me alone to say goodbye to Black Beauty.

Part Four
Riverford

Chapter Twenty-nine

There isn't much to say about my life at the White Lion – except that I missed Beauty, and I worried about him every single day.

Dick Towler was long gone, thank goodness, sacked for smoking his pipe near a load of straw just two days after the fire. Although Doris did put in a good word for me, it wasn't needed. The old ostler – Mr Hawkins – remembered how James and I had risked our lives that night, going into the burning building to save Ginger and Beauty.

"I'd be proud to have you here, lad. Proud as a king," he said.

The work was hard; I don't know how Towler had ever managed to find time to smoke his wretched pipe, let alone lean against the stable wall chattering to the customers. He must have been even lazier than I thought. I was rushed off my feet; settling strange horses for the night, feeding them, watering them and mucking out the stables so they were clean again for the new arrivals next day. Then the same process began all over again. Visitors rarely stayed more than one night, two at the most; there wasn't much to do in Riverford – except twice a year when the big horse fair was in town. Mostly, it was a stopping-off point on the way to somewhere else.

But that suited me. The visiting horses came and went. I cared for them as best as I could, but all they really needed from me was a little kindness, food, water and a dry bed. They did not need my love, and I had none to give. I had left my heart at Earlshall with Beauty. I felt hollow inside. All that was left was the empty ache in my chest.

Night-times were the worst. The other stable lads slept in the attic above the hotel, just like James and I had done on that dreadful night of the fire. But I stayed on my own in the hayloft. I liked the privacy and I wanted to be where I could hear the horses near me. If I couldn't have Beauty, then this was the next best thing. Listening to their gentle sounds in the darkness helped to soothe me a little. But still, I often did not sleep. Questions flew round and round in my head: *How was Beauty faring at Earlshall? What if Lady Magpie had made the bearing reins even tighter than before? Would James be able to keep him safe?*

Then, early one morning, after I had been at the White Lion for less than a month, I heard the sound of a horse's hooves on the stones behind me. I was mucking out a stall and had my back to the stable yard. Before I could turn my head to see who had arrived, I heard a whinny I would recognize anywhere in the world.

"Beauty?" I dropped my pitchfork and spun around. There he was – his eyes bright and his ears pricked, harnessed to the little dog cart without a bearing rein in sight.

"It's you! It's really you!" I cried, flinging my arms around his neck. I was so excited, I paid no attention at all to poor James, sitting in the dog cart grinning from ear to ear.

"I thought you might like to see an old friend," he laughed.

Beauty nuzzled me.

"Thank you," I said, looking James in the eye at last. "Thank you for bringing him here."

Before either of us could say another word, Beauty nuzzled me so hard I toppled over backwards.

The stables were quiet that morning for once, and Mr Hawkins said he could spare me for an hour or two.

James and I left the dog cart in the yard. We unharnessed Beauty and led him down to the river where he nibbled the grass while James and I sat on the bank and talked.

Although all the leaves had fallen from the trees, it was one of those beautiful wintery mornings where the sun danced through the bare branches and glistened on the water.

"Lady Magpie has gone to London," James said excitedly. "At first it was only going to be for a few days, but now the earl has business and they have decided to stay. Apparently there are lots of fashionable parties after Christmas so they are planning to be away well into the new year. Maybe even through the spring. . ."

"And they didn't want to take Beauty with them?"

"No. Nor Ginger." James gave a cheeky grin. "You cannot expect Her Royal Highness Lady Magpie to be seen driving in London with a pair of horses that do not match!"

"Well, quite!" I giggled.

I couldn't help myself, I had to leap up and throw my arms around Beauty's neck and hug him all over again.

"She can't touch you," I whispered in his silky ear. "At least until the spring." I felt my chest fill with air and realized I'd been half holding my breath ever since I left him at Earlshall.

"Mr York has gone to London to look after the stables up there," said James. "They took the two greys and the big carriage."

"Does that mean you're in charge of all the horses that have been left behind?" I asked. "Are you head groom of Earlshall while Mr York is away?"

"No." James kicked his foot against the grass. "Mr York said I could be. Even Earl Westop agreed. Then Lady Magpie stuck her nose in. She said I was too young, so they have asked Reuben Smith to fill in instead."

"Reuben Smith?" I gasped. I had seen him around Earlshall once or twice. He was a jolly sort of man who always smiled and waved, but the rumour was he had left the paddock gate open once after a night of drinking in the pub. One of the earl's finest yearlings had escaped and twisted its leg in the marsh. Now Reuben was supposed to keep away from the stables and only do odd jobs on the land.

James shrugged. "Her Ladyship hates me, ever since we argued about the bearing reins. She'd have let one of the jersey cows from the dairy be head groom rather than give me the satisfaction."

"That is not fair. . ." James was young but he was one of the most responsible people I had ever met.

"I don't mind. Not really," he said. "Reuben's a nice fellow and he hasn't touched a drop of drink for nearly three years. While he's worrying about ordering corn and paying the farrier, I can spend more time with the horses. Young Lord George is home now, and he often takes Ginger out hunting. He pushes her hard. I like to make sure she's properly cooled off and cared for when she comes back."

"So George has come home?" I asked, fresh panic swirling inside me.

"Don't worry," said James, guessing at once I'd be worried about Beauty; the rumour was that Lady Magpie's son was a terrible horseman – too rough and too fast. "He only ever rides Ginger as she is broad enough to take his weight. And, if he calls for the carriage at all, he doesn't ask for the bearing reins as he thinks they make the horses go too slow."

"There you are, you see, Beauty. Everything is going to be all right." I kissed the end of his nose and breathed a huge sigh of relief. Even if I couldn't go back to Earlshall, I knew Beauty would be safe ... for the next few months at least.

After James brought Beauty to see me, I began to sleep better at night. I often had long wonderful dreams that I was galloping over the fields on his back ... and, once, that we were racing Ginger and James on the common just like we used to.

At last I could relax, knowing Beauty was out of harm's way. But as I laid one worry to rest, something else began to trouble me.

No matter how short I cut my hair, it was getting harder and harder to disguise the fact that I was a girl. My body seemed to be changing before my very eyes. In places where I had once been skinny and straight, I now had bumps and curves. I had strange tummy aches. Worst of all, my chest had grown. I had once been as flat as any boy, but almost overnight, I grew small round bosoms which I was sure everybody could see.

I began to hunch forward, hang back in the shadows and cross my arms over my chest as much as I could. Then, one evening, as I wrapped leg bandages around a thoroughbred with a bad hock, I had a brilliant idea. I sneaked a spare roll of bandage up to the loft with me that night and wrapped it tightly around my chest to bind my bosoms flat.

"That's better," I said to myself as I pulled my waistcoat on next morning.

But it was too late.

Somebody had already noticed the changes in me.

Chapter Thirty

"I don't know what your game is," said Doris, "but something is going on!"

She had invited me round to the back of the kitchen to share a hot roll left over from the hotel guests.

"Yesterday you had 'em," she said. "And now they're gone!"

She was staring at my chest.

"Had what ... exactly?" I could feel myself blushing like a furnace as her eyes bored into me.

"Titties!" She squealed with delight. "Little ones. Like this." She dug into her apron pocket, pulled out two more bread rolls and held them up in front of her own enormous breasts. "Plain as molehills in a garden," she said, giggling. "Me and Daisy always said you was a pretty one. Well, of course you was! I've figured it out now." She poked her finger at me. "Because you, Joe Green, are a girl!"

"A girl?" My heart was beating so fast, I thought it was going to leap right out of my bandaged chest. "What nonsense!" I tried to snort in the gruffest voice I could find.

Doris just smiled. "What I want to know is what you done with 'em!" Before I could stop her, she lunged forward, pulled down the front of my shirt and peeped inside.

"Oh ... that's clever, that is!" She whistled. "Bandages!"

"Please don't tell anyone. I'll lose my job," I begged, pulling my shirt straight.

"Chambermaid's honour," Doris nodded. "But you'll have to tell me the truth."

"I – I'm not Joe Green," I whispered. What else could I say? It was over. "My name is Josephine... I'm a girl."

Then, taking both of us completely by surprise, I burst into floods of tears. "And I'm ... bleeding too ... down there." I pointed to my breeches.

"Your monthlies! Oh, Josie, you poor thing." She scooped me up into a big warm hug. "You don't mind if I call you Josie, do you?"

"No." I tried to smile, but it only made me cry even more. Nobody had called me Josie since Nanny Clay.

That evening Doris came up to the loft with a cold lamb chop, three potatoes and a dish of rice pudding with two spoons.

She also had some strips of thick cotton for me to stuff into my knickers.

"Thank you." I took the cotton gratefully.

"Tough work being a girl, ain't it?" Doris winked. "Not that you'd know much about that eh, Joe Green? You're a dark horse, you are."

Her big eyes were sparkling with excitement and I saw now why James had said she was pretty. Her whole face lit up and there was something so cheeky about her, I couldn't help but smile.

"Go on then," she said, taking a bite out of the lamb chop and passing it on to me. "I want to hear the whole story."

So I told her everything. About Father dying. Even about Mother running off to London when I was just a tiny baby. I told her how beautiful Mother had been and described the picture hanging in the nursery.

"You must miss her something terrible," said Doris.

"I just wish I'd had the chance to get to know her," I said and Doris squeezed my hand. I had never said that out loud to anyone before.

Then I told her about Aunt Lavinia and The Slug. About how they got rid of Nanny Clay and tried to send me off as a companion to Lady Hexham. How they sold all the horses. And how I escaped with Merrylegs and become a boy.

"That's how I came to Birtwick and met Black Beauty," I said. "He's all that matters to me now. He's the nearest thing to family that I have."

"I know what you mean." Doris had been quiet most of the time I was talking – only nodding her head and gasping now and then. "My old dad had this lurcher once," she said. "Terrible smelly dog it was, always farting, but… Oh my goodness!" Suddenly she leapt to her feet, her face as white as her apron.

"What is it?" I said, leaping up too and looking round. "Did you see a rat?"

Doris shook her head. "Here's me talking to you about a farting dog … and me hands are all greasy – and … and I'm chattin' away as if you was Daisy in the laundry. But you're not Daisy, are you? You're gentry…"

"No, I'm not," I said, with a grin. "Not any more

anyway. Look, my fingers are just as greasy as yours." To prove my point I picked up a cold potato, took a huge bite out of it and wiped my mouth on the back of my sleeve. The only trouble was, the bite I took was so big I began to choke on it.

"Huuh!" I spluttered and coughed, sending a shower of half-chewed potato flying through the air. A big wet chunk hit poor Doris right on the nose.

"Eww!" she squealed. But, as my spluttering turned to laughter, we both collapsed in a heap of giggles on the floor.

"I'll tell you something," Doris panted. "You ain't nothing like me and Daisy. You're common as muck you are, Lady Josephine."

"Exactly!" I giggled and we burst into fits of laughter all over again.

"Seriously, though," she said when we finally managed to calm down. "You can't go on pretending to be a lad for much longer, Josie. You're just too ... well, you just don't look like a boy no more."

"But ... but I have to be a boy," I said. "I have to work in stables ... with horses. It's the only way I'll ever have the chance to be near Black Beauty."

"Well, I don't see how that follows." Doris shrugged in her matter-of-fact way. "You ain't near him now. You might as well pull on a frilly bonnet and get yourself back to Earlspark Hall. . ."

"Earlshall Park?"

"Exactly. Get yourself back up there and see if they've got a job going in the laundry or the dairy. Then you don't have to bother with all this," she nodded at my bandaged chest. "You can nip out and see your Beauty in the stables whenever you want."

"Doris, you're brilliant!" I stared at her. Why hadn't I ever thought of that? "Although ... won't they recognize me?"

"Ha!" Doris laughed. "Believe me, Josie, nobody sees a laundry girl or a dairy maid. Not properly."

"But the servants will recognize me. Mr York. . ."

Doris made a dismissive noise. "He won't think twice. Not if you're in a dress."

"But James ... he'll definitely recognize me."

"Then why don't you just tell him?"

"I suppose I could. . ." I thought it over. If I really was going back to Earlshall, James would have to know my secret. If he knew the truth, he could help me out. "Maybe I could tell him tomorrow – he's going to be here for the horse fair."

"Is that so?" Doris sat up and pushed her hair behind her ears.

"Yes!" I felt a leap of excitement as I thought of all the different horses that would be arriving in Riverside. "He's bringing Linnet, a hunter with a big white blaze. Sir George rode her too fast, now he wants James to sell her at the fair. She's about fifteen hands high with. . ."

"Blimey! You really do natter on about nags, don't you?" Doris laughed. "What I want to know is what time you are meeting our gorgeous James Howard?"

"James? Gorgeous?" I raised my eyebrows. "If you say so." But I felt suddenly nervous. "I should be able to slip out for a bit around noon," I explained. "But Doris . . . please don't tell James I'm a girl. Not yet. I'll have to see if the moment is right – he'll be busy with the horses and – well, I think I ought to break it to him myself."

"All right!" Doris dug her spoon into the rice pudding. "Put a bit of soot on your chin, it'll look like you're growing a beard. You be Joe Green for one more day if you like. Then we'll turn you back into a girl for good."

*

"Doris!" I shouted up the stairs to the maids' rooms at the back of the hotel. "Hurry! – we're going to be late. . ." I glanced over my shoulder at the stable clock.

"All right, all right, I'm coming." Doris clattered down the steps in a pair of pointy-heeled shoes and her best Sunday frock. "*You* might not want to dress like a girl for James Howard, but some of us thought we might make a little effort."

"You look lovely," I said, trying not to giggle as I stared at her enormous hat, which was tied with an even bigger yellow ribbon.

"You don't think it's too much do you, Josie?"

"No." I stretched up and pushed the ribbons flat at the back. "There. That's perfect. But just remember, you have to call me Joe." I pulled my stable lad's cap firmly down on my own head. "I'm not Josie. Not yet."

"Got it." Doris smiled. "Come on then, J—"

"Joe!" Someone was shouting my name from the courtyard. "Joe!"

"It's James," I said. "Something's the matter."

Chapter
Thirty-one

James was standing in the courtyard. His face was as white as a sheet and his dark eyes were miserable. He was holding Linnet, Sir George's hunter, by the reins.

"Oh Joe – I'm so sorry," he said, his words tumbling out in a rush. "I didn't know they were going to take him. I tried to follow as fast as I could on Linnet, but she's lame and—"

"Slow down." I caught hold of James's arm and felt it trembling in my grip. "Who's been taken, James?"

"Beauty!" James blurted. "It's Beauty. He's gone."

"James!" Now it was me that was shaking. "I don't understand what you are saying. Start again from the beginning and, please, James, talk slowly."

"It happened the day I was last here," said James. "The day we went to the river, remember?"

"Of course I remember." James was still holding Linnet's reins but his legs were shaking so much I led him over to the water trough and made him perch on the edge. I was desperate to find out more but I tried not to rush him.

"It was just getting dark when we arrived back at Earlshall that night," said James. "I cleaned Beauty down, fed him and put him in his stall as usual. It was only then that I noticed none of the other horses seemed to have any hay or fresh water. I asked if any of the farm lads had seen Reuben Smith, seeing as he was supposed to be in charge. But the lads said no – they hadn't seen him since lunchtime."

"He'd been drinking again?" I guessed.

James swallowed. "I'm so sorry, Joe. I tended to the horses and went to bed myself." He shook his head. "I-I had no idea Reuben would come back and take Beauty for a ride. It was the middle of the night – pitch black for goodness' sake."

"He rode Beauty? Drunk?" The panic rose to my throat.

James took a deep breath. "Reuben had been drinking all afternoon in the King's Head. When they finally threw him out, he said if they wouldn't take his money, he'd fetch a horse from the stables and ride to the Rusty Nail in Upton instead."

"But that's ten miles away. On a horrible broken road." We had gone towards Upton once with Lady Magpie in the carriage. She had banged on the ceiling telling James to go faster even though the horses had to pick their way over the stones. "He took Beauty there? In the dark?" I asked in disbelief.

"Not all the way." James shook his head "They never made it."

"What do you mean?" I said. "What do you mean they never made it, James?"

"First thing I knew about it was when I woke in the middle of the night," said James. "The horses were restless, I could hear them fretting. As soon as I went down I saw Beauty was gone. I thought for a minute it might be you, Joe. I thought perhaps you'd come back and stolen him after all."

Oh, how I wish I had.

"I took a lantern and ran to the gate," said James. "That's when I saw Ged Herr, the landlord from the King's Head. He was worried Reuben was in no fit state to ride a horse and he'd run all the way from the village to warn me. But it was too late."

James told us how he had harnessed Ginger to the dog cart and he and Ged Herr had driven as fast as they dared towards Upton.

"We'd only just passed the turnpike when we saw them," James said. "Reuben was lying on the ground and Beauty was standing over him, with his head bent. I – I untangled Beauty's reins while Ged went over to Reuben." James looked up at me. "He was dead, Joe. His neck was broken – he must have been galloping flat out when he fell."

"And Beauty?" I gasped. I knew I should feel something for poor dead Reuben Smith, but all I could think about was Beauty. My precious horse.

"He was missing a shoe," said James slowly. "And his knees were ripped to shreds."

"He fell?" I felt sick.

"Must have done." James nodded. "Reuben rode him like a lunatic. I could see that from the way he was sweating and shivering. I think he must have stumbled on the sharp stones and Reuben flew right over his head."

"But-but this happened weeks ago. Why didn't you tell me?"

"I didn't want to worry you," said James miserably.

"I hoped Beauty's knees would get better. And they have ... they've mended brilliantly. But they're scarred for ever."

I felt a twisting pain inside me.

"That's the problem," said James. "Sir George says his mother won't have a carriage horse with scars on his knees."

"No," I said slowly. "I don't suppose she would."

"Sure enough, Lady Magpie ordered he was to be sold," said James. "But I never thought it would be so soon. I thought they'd give him more time to recover. But the dealer was passing through on his way to the fair – he came at the crack of dawn this morning and just rode Beauty away..."

"Wait! Beauty is to be sold? At the horse fair? Today?" I stared while James nodded helplessly. "We have to find him," I cried.

James thrust Linnet's reins at Doris, who was standing in the doorway to the inn. "Look after her. Joe – wait for me."

I was already running under the stable arch and out into the crowded market place beyond.

I had to find Black Beauty before he was sold to a stranger and disappeared from my life for ever.

Chapter Thirty-two

There were horses everywhere.

Normally I would have loved every second of the fair. Pens of three or four little ponies and groups of coloured cobs filled the market square. Huge shires with shining brass on their harnesses thundered up and down the road. There were thoroughbreds and farm horses, brood mares and geldings; coats in every shade of chestnut, grey, bay and dun.

But all I was looking for was a glimpse of black. The rich dark ebony I knew so well.

Nothing.

"And now," cried a man with a clanging handbell. "I pronounce the Riverford Winter Horse Fair open. Sales may begin."

The town was thronged with buyers, dealers, grooms and stable lads – everyone seemed to be dressed in tweed or brown corduroy, hollering numbers at each other beside the horse pens.

"Twenty-three pounds for the dapple grey."

"Twenty-two ten and not another sixpence."

"Done."

The noise was deafening. Horses neighed, calling for lost owners and missing friends. Men shouted and hustled. Two yearling colts kicked each other and squealed. Two young men punched each other and rolled on the ground outside the Rose and Crown.

I leapt over them and dashed down River Street, my heart pounding.

"Beauty, where are you?"

On the corner by the churchyard, a blacksmith had set up a makeshift furnace to fit horses with new shoes. I felt the blazing heat flush my cheeks as I ducked past and the clang of his anvil echoed through my ears. Beside him, a saddler hammered studs into leather bridles, harnesses and reins.

"Excuse me," I panted, "have you seen a black horse with a white star?"

"Couldn't say." The saddler shrugged.

I pelted on towards the river.

As I crossed the bridge, I stopped for a moment to catch my breath. Looking across the low-lying fields I saw that the pens here were more spread out. Instead of ruddy-faced farmers, gentlemen strolled across the grass.

I passed a beautiful brood mare, her belly round with a new foal. She had a fine head and bright eyes. And there were two strong hunters in the pen behind her. Then a pair of dappled grey carriage horses...

"Nice, aren't they?" said the dealer, catching my eye. "You get a better class of horse down here by the river. Not like the riff-raff up in the town."

"Is that true?" I asked, with a surge of fresh hope.

"Reckon so," said the dealer, turning to smile at a gentleman who was examining the greys. "Have you ever seen a finer pair to pull a carriage, sir?"

I dashed on across the field, hoping with every step that I would see Black Beauty. But there was still no sign of him.

I saw the flick of a black tail. But it was just a bay gelding.

A coachman in a mustard-yellow coat was haggling with the dealer.

"Seventeen pounds and I'll take him," he said.

"Seventeen? Don't insult me." The dealer spat on

the ground. "If that's all the money you've got, head down to the tannery. That's where the broken old nags can be found."

"Broken?" Suddenly I remembered the wounds on Beauty's legs. But surely he still belonged here, amongst the fine horses.

"Lame, sick, stubborn. So long as you're not fussy you can get yourself any kind of bargain in Tanner's Yard," said the dealer. "Pumice foot, fallen pasterns, capped hock, ewe neck, quarter crack, mange, megrims, heaves, poll evil ... worms, warts and windgalls. They can all be yours."

"Scarred knees?" I asked.

"Now the lad gets my drift," said the dealer, laughing. "If that's the sort of broken beast you want, head down Tanner's Yard with the horse-meat butchers and the knackers' boys. Otherwise, I'll hear a serious offer for this fine bay gelding."

"Nineteen pounds..." offered the coachman as I sped away.

Butchers? Could my poor, proud Black Beauty really be sold for meat?

I ran back over the bridge, heading for the terrible-sounding Tanner's Yard, as fast as my legs could carry me.

"James!" I saw him darting round the corner by the blacksmith's forge. "Have you found Beauty?"

"No. We better try Tanner's," he shouted over the sound of the hammering. We'd obviously both had the same horrible idea. "But Joe" – he tried to grab my arm – "what will you do if you find him?"

I shook him off. I couldn't answer that; all I knew was that I had to find Beauty and soon. I would reveal my true identity – tell people I was the daughter of a baronet; I would beg, borrow and steal the money if I had to. But I must have Beauty.

We dived into a narrow alleyway behind the saddlery and were soon in the dark cobbled lanes that lead towards the town tannery.

"A dealer said the horses down here might be sold for meat," I said, panting. "Is that true?"

James said nothing as we ran on past a poor old donkey with a belly so low it almost touched the ground.

"James?" I panted. "Is it true?"

"Sometimes." James nodded.

"Not Beauty, though." I kept on running. "I don't care if his knees are scarred. No one would do that to him. They'd see how fine he is. I know they would."

We hurtled round the corner in to Tanner's Yard.

It was a big square space overlooked on four sides by the high brick walls of the tanning factory. The air smelt thick and strangely sweet.

There were three long rows of crowded horse pens, all surrounded by groups of shouting men. Wordlessly, James and I split up to look.

I glanced into every pen I passed but could see at once that these horses were not Beauty. The atmosphere here was very different. The animals all looked shabby and tattered. Some were very old, some young and badly used. But some pricked their ears and watched me as I raced by.

"I'm looking for something steady to ride about my parish," said a vicar, talking to a dealer with an old white cob.

"Then Moses here is your fellow. Steady as Sunday morning, so he is," the dealer said and chuckled. And I felt a tiny lift of hope. Even in my panic for Beauty, I was pleased to know some of the horses here would get a second chance.

"Excuse me," I slid to a halt, "I'm looking for a horse. . ."

"Well, you've come to the right place, lad. This is a horse fair." The dealer chuckled even louder than before. "But I think the vicar has first choice on Moses. . ."

"No, I mean a special horse," I said.

"Now hang on. Are you saying my old Moses isn't specia—"

"A black horse," I interrupted. "Beautiful. With a white star right in the middle of his forehead. And one white sock." My eyes were filling with tears. "I think he may have ruined knees."

"Ah, yes!" the dealer scratched his chin. "Proper bargain, that one. Saw him myself this morning . . . magnificent creature. Just a shame about them scars."

"You saw him?" My tummy turned a somersault. "Where?" I cried. "Where did you see him?"

"Just there. Middle row, about halfway down." The dealer pointed towards the centre of Tanner's Yard. "You can't miss him. He's right next to the pen with the three mules."

I saw the mules at once. Their long ears were poking up in the air.

But the pen next to them was empty.

A short man with wiry hair like a terrier was throwing brushes and a rope halter into an empty bucket.

This had to be the dealer.

"Where's Beauty? Where's the black horse from Earlshall?" I asked, my voice cracking.

"Sold." The man jumped from foot to foot excitedly. "Gone for a pretty price too. Twenty-four pounds and ten shillings. I couldn't have got better than that. Not with those scarred knees."

"Who did you sell him to?" I cried. "Not to a butcher? Please not a butcher!"

"For that money? Don't be daft." The man gave a shrill laugh. "He's gone to London to be a cab horse. Barker: that was the name of the fellow that brought him. Or was it Baker? Yes, I'd swear on my old ma's life it was Baker."

"When?" I asked. "How long since you sold him?"

"Not five minutes ago." The dealer pointed down the road that led out of town. He saw my face. "You might catch him if you're quick."

I turned and ran, ran through the streets to the London road. For a moment I thought I saw Beauty, disappearing behind a milk cart, but as I got closer, he was gone. If he was ever there, he had vanished again like a shadow in the crowd. There was just an old woman and a donkey, plodding away down the long empty road towards London. Nothing. Desperately I scanned the horizon, but I knew it was no good.

Black Beauty was gone.

Chapter
Thirty-three

James and I spent another hour combing the market square and Tanner's Yard in case Beauty was still nearby. I even went as far as the fields by the river. But I knew it was hopeless.

"There's nothing for it," I said at last. "I'm going to London."

"You're – what?" asked James, startled.

"Going to London," I said. "That's where Beauty is. I'm going now."

"You'll never find him in London. There are so many horses," said James. "It's a huge city. . ."

"I've got to try." I turned and walked towards the White Lion.

"But. . ." James caught at my arm. "Joe, that's

madness."

"Don't worry," I spun around and faced him again, "I'm not asking you to come with me. You can go back to your precious Earlshall and..."

"Earlshall is not precious to me!" James's face flushed. "I hate it there as much as you did. But I have to go back. I have to sell Linnet at the fair today and take the money to Sir George. I have responsibilities..."

"Responsibilities? To that horrible family?"

"Yes," said James. "I am a servant. That is what I do, Joe ... I serve! And, unless you have forgotten, Ginger is still there too. I have to go back and look after her."

"Go on then," I said, anger spitting out of me. I knew it wasn't James's fault that Beauty had been injured, not his fault that he had been sold; but I had no one else to blame and now all my fury was turned on him. "You promised me you'd take care of Beauty. You *promised* me. I just hope you make a better job of looking after Ginger than you did of looking after Black Beauty for me."

"Joe..." James stumbled back as if I had punched him. "If I could turn back time, I would."

"Well you can't," I said, as I stormed through the arch into the White Lion courtyard. "Neither of us can.

But if you've got any sense you'll save Ginger before it's too late. Get her away from Earlshall, James."

I pointed to poor lame Linnet, tied in a stall.

"That's what happened to the last horse Sir George rode," I said. "Save Ginger, James." The words stuck in my throat. "Save her before it's too late, like it was for Beauty."

"Joe, I'm so sorry. . ."

"Sorry won't bring Beauty back," I said.

I spun on my heel and walked away.

I wish now that I had been more kind.

I wish I had told him what happened to Beauty was not his fault. It was Reuben Smith. And beer. And the cruelty of Lady Magpie who would not keep a carriage horse with scars on his knees.

I wish I had told him he was my friend.

But, by the time I climbed down from the loft with my little bag of belongings, Linnet's stall was empty. She was gone. And so was James.

I told no one I was leaving except Doris. She listened as I explained and then took my hand.

"I won't stop you going, Josie; I can see it's not worth me trying. But I want to give you something." She led me upstairs to the little white bedroom she shared with four other maids. "Don't worry," she said, seeing my anxious face. "There's no one about. They've all gone to flirt with grooms at the horse fair." She pushed open the door. "There!"

She pointed a pile of clothes on the end of her bed. I could see a white pinafore and a brown smock dress. *Girls'* clothes.

"They don't fit me any more, but there's still plenty of wear in them."

"They look perfect," I said, eyeing them nervously. It had been so long since I had worn skirts.

"It'll be a lot easier for you to travel as a girl now that you're growing so womanly." She folded her arms. "Just try them on."

"Fine!" I sighed, slipping my shirt off, untying the bandages around my chest and pulling the brown dress over my head.

"Here. Let me do that," said Doris, as I fumbled to tie a bow in the back of the pinafore. "You're just out of practice, that's all."

"Thank you." I didn't like to tell her that Nanny Clay had always tied my pinafore for me.

"Oh, my word! If Daisy saw you now, she'd faint like a feather!" Doris smiled, spinning me round so that I could see myself in the little chipped looking glass above the dressing table. "There you are."

And there I was. Josie Green. A girl again. I didn't recognize myself – a thin tanned face, with wide green eyes, thick lashes, and curves beneath the pinafore. Not a stable boy any more – but not a fine lady either.

I was still staring in shock when I heard Doris gasp, "Oh, that hair! It'll never do. Here. You better take this." She lifted the hat with the big yellow ribbons from her own head.

"No, Doris!" I cried. "It's your Sunday best."

"We can't have you looking scruffy in London." She pulled the hat down until it almost covered my eyes. It was so big, I felt like I was wearing a washtub on my head . . . all tied up with a bright yellow ribbon.

But Doris was right. I did need something to cover my boyish hair. And, in that moment, I made a decision. I would travel to London as a girl. "Thank you, it's perfect." I kissed Doris goodbye as she helped me into an old faded coat of hers, and then stamped my feet into Billy's big boots. They would just have to do. And no one would see them under my long skirt.

I stepped out of the door and into the courtyard.

"Excuse me," I asked an old man with a draper's cart. "Are you going to London?"

Part Five
London

Chapter Thirty-four

I hung out of the side of the draper's cart all the way to London, hoping that I would catch sight of Beauty on the road.

"Has your sweetheart run away, miss?" the old draper Mr Silver teased me.

"Leave the poor girl alone," said his wife.

When I told them I was looking for a beautiful black horse who had been sold by mistake, they promised to keep an eye out too.

But we never caught up with Beauty on the road.

"It doesn't matter," I told myself over and over again. "I'll find him." *At least I know he is going to be a cab horse,* I thought. *That is a good start.*

As we drew close to London though, my heart sank.

It was twilight and the gas lamps were already lit. The main road into the city was crowded with carriages and carts. We had to stop and start and stop and start again, until we came to a standstill in a queue on a big bridge over the wide grey River Thames.

I had never seen so many horses in my whole life.

There was no way through and nothing to do but wait. Yet, still, people shouted and jostled. Whips cracked and horses stamped their feet.

Poor Beauty. He had never known anything but open fields and quiet lanes.

"I do hope the cab man is kind," I whispered. "I hope *he* does not crack his whip."

"Where should I drop you?" said Mr Silver, when we were over the bridge at last.

"Could you take me to where the cabs are?" I asked.

"But there's horse cabs everywhere!" said old Mrs Silver.

"Oh, I know," I said. "But where are the horses kept at night?"

I imagined there must be an enormous stable

where all the cab horses were cared for, ready to go to work in the morning.

"They live all over the place," said Mr Silver. "Each cab driver looks after his own horse, sometimes two. And then there is a few big cab companies who own lots of horses and loan them out to the drivers one by one."

"But..." I felt sick to my stomach. I could see streets and streets of higgledy-piggledy houses stretching out on either side of us. Not to mention butchers' shops and builders' yards, bakeries and costermongers' stalls. Black Beauty could be anywhere. It was impossible. James had tried to warn me and it was true; I would never find Beauty in this city. Never.

The old couple were having a whispered conversation and now Mrs Silver put an arm around my shoulders. "Listen, my dear. You come home with us, get a good night's sleep and start your hunt in the morning."

"Oh, but—"

"Ain't no point arguing with my Molly," said Mr Silver. "And anyway, that horse of yours will be tucked up with a nice bran mash after a journey like he's had from Riverford today."

"Of course." Suddenly what the kind draper said

made sense. Beauty wouldn't be out on the streets, not now. He'd be in a stable somewhere, eating his evening meal.

I realized how hungry I was then, and tired too.

"You come home with us, love," said Mrs Silver as my tummy rumbled loudly. "We'll get you a nice bowl of warm soup and a safe dry bed for the night."

"Thank you!" As the grey fog swirled around the London streets I was pleased to have found somewhere to spend my first night alone in the big city. My spirits lifted a little. It would be light in the morning and I could begin my search then.

"Don't worry, Beauty," I whispered in the darkness. "I haven't given up. I'll find you. Tomorrow..."

In the morning, Mr Silver showed me where to catch the horse-drawn omnibus to St Pancras station.

Luckily, although I had left before my last wages were due, I had a little money saved. I paid my fare and climbed the iron stairs up to the open deck on top.

"You take care, young lady," called Mr Silver.

"Thank you." I waved as the three strong horses pulling the enormous omnibus trotted away.

When I climbed down at the busy station, I saw

the line of hansom cabs at once. Each high-wheeled buggy was pulled by one horse, with a hood and window for the passengers, while the driver sat on a high box at the back, looking over the roof where he held the long reins.

But it wasn't the cabs I was looking at. It was the horses – they seemed half-starved and ragged. My heart sank as I desperately searched the line for Beauty.

"Excuse me," I called up to the nearest driver "Could you tell me where I might find a fine black horse?"

"What?" he shouted above the noise of the trains. "Climb in, so long as you can pay the fare."

He peered down at my shabby brown frock.

"I don't want to go anywhere," I said, "I just want to ask you a question if I may. . ."

"Questions are for school. Step out of the way," snapped the driver.

A man in a fine grey coat barged me aside as he rushed from a train.

"Harley Street, and quick as you can," he shouted, climbing inside the cab and bashing on the roof with his stick.

"Right you are, governor." The driver cracked his

whip and his skinny grey gelding stumbled on his way.

I looked down the line again in horror. The next three horses were just as thin. They hung their heads and their eyes were clouded.

The fourth horse was the worst of all – an old black mare – her coat almost as dark as Beauty's but dull as stone. She was so thin I could count her ribs like the railings on a iron fence.

Was this what cab horses were like? Was this what Beauty would become?

I almost sank down on the pavement I was so afraid.

"Are you all right there, lassie?"

A Scottish-sounding man with a big red beard called out to me from the other side of the street.

He was a cab driver too, but was standing at his horse's head while she ate from a nosebag, hooked to the bottom of her bridle.

I smiled with relief as I saw that his horse, at least – a big strong roan mare – was plump with a shining coat.

"I–I'm looking for a horse," I said. "Please, can you help me?"

Chapter
Thirty-five

I told the Scotsman about Beauty and he explained that the thin horses I had seen all belonged to the big cab companies, who hired them out to the drivers for a fee.

"The drivers work the poor brutes flat out to get the most out of their money they can. They don't look after them, because they can hire a different horse when the first one is all used up. It's a terrible business."

"How horrible," I said, as another thin gelding rattled past pulling a cab with his head hung low.

"Not like Pinky, here. I own her myself so it's in my interest to feed her well and see that she's not overworked," he said. "I don't want the poor lass getting sick. If she does, I'll have no one to pull my cab. And besides, Pinky is like a friend to me."

"I can see that," I said as he undid the nosebag and the roan mare rubbed her head against the driver.

"This black horse of yours," he said. "He sounds like he's been bought by an owner, for sure; the cab companies wouldn't go all that way just to buy a horse at the fair."

"So the man who bought Beauty will look after him well?" I said.

"Sure to." The Scotsman smiled as he led Pinky over to join the line of waiting cabs.

"I think the man's name is Baker or Barker. You don't know him, do you?" I said, following them across the road. If Nanny Clay was here she would say I was "pestering" but I had to find out as much as I could.

"Sorry, lass," he shrugged. "There are over ten thousand cabbies. . ."

"Ten thousand?" I gasped. "All here in London?" How was I supposed to find Beauty's driver among that many? I didn't even know his name for sure.

"Is this station a good place to start, at least?" I

asked, hope slipping away like water from a cracked jug.

"Yes." The driver smiled kindly. "You might be lucky here. Or try Euston, or Paddington, or Bishopsgate. Any of the big stations."

He was at the front of the queue now and a grand woman in a large lavender hat appeared from the platform.

"To the opera house," she said. "In Covent Garden."

"Right you are." The cabby touched his hat to me. "Goodbye, lassie."

The lady climbed inside the cab, turning sideways to fit her enormous hat through the door.

"They call me Mac by the way," the driver called as Pinky trotted away. "If I see this Black Beauty of yours, I'll let you know."

"Thank you!" I smiled and waved as brightly as I could, but a flood of loneliness washed over me as soon as he was around the corner.

I was just plucking up courage to go and speak to the next driver in line, when Mac's loud voice startled me. "Lassie!" He was back. "Hop up here," he cried, pointing to the space beside him on the high box seat above the cab. "I've had an idea."

"What are you doing, driver?" The brim of the lavender hat poked out of the window. "Why have you returned to the station? This is where I came from, you silly man."

"Right you are, madam," called Mac as I scrambled up to the seat beside him.

"I want to go to the opera, you fool," the lady barked.

"And so you shall." Mac didn't bat an eyelid at being insulted. "Come on, Pinky, lass," he said turning the horse's head around. "I always have terrible trouble getting her to go to the opera," he called down. "She's more for the ballet, my Pinky."

I giggled as a picture of the little tubby mare wearing a frilly dance tutu popped into my mind.

"So, here's my thinking, lass," he said, when we both stopped laughing. "There's so many different railway stations nowadays, with cabbies waiting outside each one, you'd always be playing a game of cat and mouse. Maybe while you were back there at St Pancras, your Black Beauty would be at Bishopsgate. Or while you were at Paddington he'd have set off for King's Cross."

"I suppose so," I said, my head swimming.

"What you need to do is to stay in one place, lassie," he said. "That's how a cat catches the wee mouse. She stays by the hole!"

"The hole?"

"Covent Garden! That's the mouse hole," said Mac. He waved his hands like a magician as we turned the corner into a huge bustling market place.

"It's so beautiful," I cried in surprise. And it was. There were flower sellers on every corner and carts laden with cabbages and carrots, turnips and cauliflowers in broad stripes of green and orange and white. The colours looked so bright against the grey London streets and cold winter sky.

"Wait until the summer, it's like a bonny meadow," said Mac. "Strawberries, peaches, roses . . . daffodils in the spring."

"I'd love to see that," I said. "But I don't want to be here in the summer. I want to have found Black Beauty by then."

We had stopped in front of a building with tall pillars like a Roman temple.

"Opera house," called Mac and the lavender lady climbed down from the cab.

"I hope you don't expect a tip, because you are not getting one!" she sniffed.

"As you wish." Mac took his fare and bowed politely as the lady stomped away. "Now, lass. There's Drury Lane with all the theatres that way, and the Strand with cafes and restaurants just down the road. This is the beating heart of London. Every cabby comes to Covent Garden sooner or later. If you wait here long enough you'll see your Black Beauty trot by."

"Like a cat at a mouse hole?" I said.

"Exactly!" Mac grinned. "I'll have to leave you to it, lassie. But good luck."

"Thank you," I called, scrambling down from the cab. Mac had changed everything. It wasn't hopeless. I could find Beauty. All I had to do was watch and wait.

Chapter Thirty-six

Five days I sat on the steps outside the opera. A thousand cabs must have trotted past me or pulled up on the kerb to drop fine ladies in winter furs and gentlemen in smart top hats.

But not one of the cabs was pulled by Beauty.

"Move along! You're like a stray dog sitting there on the steps like that," said the usher outside the theatre.

"I'm not a dog. I'm a cat," I said, remembering how Mac had told me to stay watching in one place and never move. "Only I'm waiting to catch a horse, not a mouse."

"A horse-catching cat! I've heard it all now!" The usher laughed. "But at least you've made me smile."

After that he let me stay, bringing me bitter cups of hot coffee and only pretending to bustle me along when the theatre manager came by.

It turned out he was called Arthur and had grown up in the country near Newmarket.

"I dreamed of being a jockey until I grew tall as a beanstalk," he said with a grin.

I told him exactly what Beauty looked like. "I'll keep my eyes peeled," he promised.

Nights were the busiest times of all. The cabs dropped off the opera-goers in time for the show, or hurried past on the way to the theatres on Drury Lane. They came and went between restaurants and cafes and swarmed back again at the end of the night to take people home. All the time, I kept watching, looking, hoping to see Beauty somewhere in the swirl of traffic. Sometimes I thought of Mother – wondering whether she was out there too, somewhere in that glittering throng. Would we even recognize each other if we were to pass in the crowd? Probably not; all I had to remember her by was that one picture with those bright green eyes. All she knew was the tiny baby she had left so long ago.

At last, about one o'clock in the morning, the streets grew quiet and no more cabs and horses came. Then I would slip away and huddle under an old vegetable wagon or a market stall. After the first night, I learnt quickly to keep out of sight, well away from policemen and drunks and lonely men seeking the company of the women who walked the streets at night. I curled myself into a little ball, covered up with a piece of old sack from a turnip bag and dozed fitfully until the lamplighter came to put the gaslights out at dawn. Then the day began again.

Sometimes I cried, thinking how much I missed Beauty and how afraid I was. But mostly I tried to stay brave. I longed for a hot meal, but Arthur's cups of coffee kept me warm and there was plenty of fruit – apples, carrots, maybe a raw potato – that fell from the stalls during the day. I remembered how Wilf at Birtwick had longed to come to London. Like Dick Whittington, he thought the streets would be paved with gold. The twins would laugh to find there wasn't any gold at all, just vegetables like they grew in the garden at home.

"You want to watch it, Josie," said Arthur, on my sixth day. "You're getting awful thin. You'll be like the Crawlers soon."

"No I won't," I cried. Crawlers were old women mostly; so poor, they were little more than heaps of rag and bone, too tired, thin and weak to even beg. Sometimes they barely moved all day. They shifted only to crawl left or right when kicked like a dog to get out of someone's way. How they stayed alive I had no idea.

"I'll tell you something else," said Arthur, "there'll be snow soon."

He was right. On my seventh day it came.

I was woken that morning not by the sound of sellers setting up their stalls, but by the sound of bells.

"Of course, it's Sunday," I said as the song of London's churches rang out. The market would be closed today. I shivered, climbing out from under a vegetable wagon, muttering the old nursery rhyme Nanny Clay had taught me.

> *Oranges and lemons,*
> *Say the bells of St.Clement's.*

> *You owe me five farthings,*
> *Say the bells of St. Martin's. . .*

I stopped, halfway out, and gasped. The world had turned white.

A great blanket of fresh snow was spread all across Covent Garden market.

"Oooh!" I couldn't resist... I was just about to run across the square to be the first to christen the new snow with my footprints when I noticed that there was already a set of markings after all... I saw horseshoe prints and the wheels of a cab. Just one set. Very faint – as if they had been left by a ghost while I was sleeping.

I buttoned my coat and began to follow, drawn along as if the tracks were trying to lead me somewhere.

Beauty? I thought. *Beauty. Is this you?*

The tracks led on, still just one horse and one set of wheels, down Bow Street past the Theatre Royal and into Drury Lane. My heart was pounding. Without knowing quite why, I began to run, glancing left and right but the streets were empty.

"Hello?" I shouted out, but my voice just echoed back to me, quiet and strangely muffled by the snow.

I ran on, slipping and sliding on the icy cobbles, desperate to catch sight of the horse that had left the tracks.

"Whoa!" As I reached the junction with Wych

Street, a carriage shot out from the side road, and I only just stopped myself from colliding with it. "Watch where you're going, girl!" cried the coachman, cracking his whip at me as his team of four greys thundered away down Drury Lane.

I stumbled backwards and sat in the snow. The single track of hoof prints was ruined now, smudged and smoothened by skidding wheels and the fresh marks of the speeding team of four.

Swoosh! A high buggy pulled by a chestnut mare came the other way. I had to pull my knees up tight as the driver swerved to miss my feet.

Then it was quiet again and I sat still in the road, trying to catch my breath for a moment more.

As my breathing steadied, I had a strange feeling I was being watched. My spine tingled. I looked around but there was no one; just the silent, snowy streets.

I dusted myself off, trying to shake the odd feeling. Then, as I looked up, I saw a poster on the wall above me.

THE BARD THEATRE, DRURY LANE

Antony and Cleopatra by William Shakespeare.

The poster showed the famous Egyptian queen in the arms of the Roman general. Her hair was jet black, as dark as Beauty's tail and she wore a golden crown in the shape of a snake. She looked so romantic, beautiful and proud. And her eyes. . .

I gasped. Those eyes. The same eyes that had stared down at me from the nursery wall every day of my life at Summer's Place.

I did not need to read the name on the poster.

Starring Valentina Green.

I knew who it was.

It was Mother.

Chapter Thirty-seven

I was still staring up at the poster when I heard a horse whinny and someone calling my name.

"There you are, Josie, lass," said Mac as Pinky picked her way down the snowy street. "We've been looking all over for you."

"Mac!" I gasped, tearing my eyes away from the poster. "Have you heard something? Have you found Beauty?"

"I can't promise," said Mac with a big grin. "But jump up and we'll go and see."

"You think Beauty's in Richmond?" I said.

We were trotting along near the river, through the quiet Sunday streets of London. Pinky was pulling a little light trap instead of the heavy hansom cab and we fairly sped along. I gasped as I saw Big Ben and the Houses of Parliament glistening with snow. "Like the old city's put on a wedding dress," Mac said.

Then he told me how he had heard news of a cab horse south of the river who fitted Beauty's description.

"Owned by a fellow by the name of Brannigan."

"That could be him!" I cried. "Barker, Baker . . . Brannigan." At least it began with the right letter.

"I don't ken him myself," said Mac. "Folk say he's not a bad sort. A bit gruff perhaps. But rumour is the horse is as black as midnight."

As Pinky's bit jingled and the wheels of the trap rattled over the snow, I began to sing a little tune inside my head: *Let it be Beauty. Let it be Beauty. Let it be Beauty. Please.*

Brannigan was a big man who lived in a tiny cottage, tucked away in a ramshackle street close to the river. He appeared at the door still chewing his breakfast and it took a while before he understood my garbled plea to see his horse.

"You want to look at Blackie?" he growled and scratched his chin.

"Just a quick peek," I said. "That's all we'll need." I would know in an instant if it was Beauty or not.

"And what if he is this horse of yours?" said Brannigan. "What good will that do you? I paid good money for that nag." He folded his arms and stood like a rock.

"Where did you buy him?" I asked. "From Riverford Fair?"

"Riverford? No," scoffed Brannigan. "I got him from a dealer in Windsor."

"Oh." My heart sank a little but Mac squeezed my shoulder.

"You only got him two days ago. Is that right?" he asked Brannigan.

"Thursday." Brannigan nodded.

"So he could still be this wee lassie's horse," Mac explained. "The fellow who brought him in Riverford could've passed him on to your fellow in Windsor, who sold him to you and. . ."

While they were talking, I noticed a shed at the end of the street with a muck heap behind it. Brannigan's horse must be inside. I crept away. Could it really be Beauty? I had to find out for sure.

It was black as a cave inside the shed.

I could hear the horse shifting his feet and breathing somewhere in the darkness.

"Beauty?" I whispered. "Beauty, is that you?"

But even before his soft nose touched my hand, I knew.

This horse was not Beauty.

He did not sound like Beauty. He did not smell like Beauty. And, as I buried my head in his short scruffy mane, he did not feel like Beauty either.

"I wish you were," I said. "But you're not."

Even so, I couldn't let go. It felt good to hold him and I stayed, whispering in his ears, until Brannigan flung open the door of the shed.

As winter light flooded in, I saw that the horse did not look like Beauty either. Blackie had a long, heavy head like a cow with small ears and big teeth. He seemed gentle and kind but his coat was dull and his legs were short. He was not Black Beauty. Not even close.

"Sorry, lass," said Mac miserably. "I thought it was worth a shot."

"It was. It really was. And it was so kind of you to take me," I said, trying to sound cheerful as we sloshed and slithered our way back towards the city. Poor Pinky kept slipping on the slushy streets.

The snow on the ground had turned grey and wet, churned up by horses and cartwheels all day long. And it had begun to sleet now too, thick wet drops blown in our faces by the wind.

"I'd planned to come back past Buckingham Palace," said Mac. "I thought a country lass like you might like to see the sights. But are you not in the mood for it?"

"Oh please do, I should love to see," I said. Sad as I was I couldn't bear for Mac to notice, not after all he had tried to do. He was such a kind man.

"You never know," I said, attempting to laugh. "If Queen Victoria is home, she might invite us in for a cup of tea."

"And a shortbread biscuit, I hope," chuckled Mac.

But the palace just looked big and grey and cold. If there was anyone at home, the sleet was falling far too thick and fast by then for us to even see the windows.

"Where will you sleep tonight?" Mac asked.

I coughed and tried not to answer.

"You can't stay out on the streets, Josie. Not in weather like this," he said. "I'd invite to you to stay at mine if I could. But it's my uncle's lodgings – just two rooms – and I've three big cousins all as rough as rams. I don't think it's any place for a lassie."

"I'll be fine, Mac," I said, pulling Doris's old coat up around my neck. "Honestly I will."

"I don't like it," muttered Mac. "I've a wee sister your age back in Scotland. I'd hate to think of her out on the streets in the cold all night."

He was right. The thought of crawling under an old fruit wagon again tonight was almost more than I could bear. Seeing Blackie had made me realize again how hopeless my search for Beauty was.

I shivered, more with misery than cold.

Even if I did not freeze to death tonight, I would never find my Beauty. London was just too big. Too busy. And too lonely. How could I hope to find a horse in a place so huge that people barely knew each other's names?

Then I thought of Mac, sitting beside me, his face looking so sad, all because he was worried for me.

Just a week ago, Mac had been a stranger too. I hadn't known his name. Or Pinky's. Now here they were. Out on a Sunday. In the snow. Just to try and make my dream of finding Beauty come true.

'You don't have to worry about me, Mac," I said

in a cheerful voice. "I know we couldn't find Beauty today, but . . . but I did find someone else."

"Who?" asked Mac, his face brightening almost at once. "Who did you find, lass?"

I thought of the poster of Cleopatra and a strange fluttering feeling flickered in the pit of my tummy.

"Someone special," I said as Mac's grin grew even broader. "This morning, on Drury Lane . . . I found my mother."

Chapter Thirty-eight

Mac dropped me outside the Bard Theatre, right underneath the poster of Cleopatra.

"Are you sure you'll be all right, lass?" he asked for the hundredth time.

"Don't you worry, Mother's meeting me here in half an hour," I lied. "You get Pinky home for a nice bran mash."

"As long as you're sure."

"I'm sure," I said. Without my fib, I think Mac would have kept poor Pinky standing there in the cold all night. But at last they trotted away into the dusk, waving as they went.

As it was, the theatre was all closed up, of course, because it was Sunday. And so began the longest night of my life. I daren't keep still, for fear I'd freeze, so instead I walked. First to the end of Drury Lane. Then back to the Bard Theatre. Then to the opera house. Then back to the Bard again. Then from the Bard to the river. Then back to the Bard, always stopping under the gas lamp outside the theatre to stare into Mother's Cleopatra eyes.

The eyes stared back at me – so bright I almost believed the poster would come alive.

"Mother?" I stretched out my hand and touched the cold paper. Cleopatra didn't even blink, of course.

I couldn't keep still for long. Off I went, walking again.

I didn't sleep at all that night. Up and down the quiet Sunday streets I tramped. The sleet had left off and it was a beautiful clear crisp night. But questions tumbled around my brain like snowflakes.

Should I go to the theatre when it opened?

Should I speak to Mother?

Would she recognize me?

Would she want to see me?

Why did she run away?

Why did she leave me all those years ago?

Exhausted, I found myself outside St Martin's

church at five o'clock in the morning. The darkness was still velvet-thick but the city was coming back to life. It was Monday.

"What should I do?" I said out loud. I didn't know if I was asking God or Beauty or talking to myself. I sank down on the church steps as the bells chimed the hour. When I looked up a fresh flurry of snow was falling. I watched as the world turned white and beautiful again, all the slush covered over. My spirits lifted. "It's like a new start!" I said and I leapt to my feet, leaving a trail of fresh footprints, as I ran towards the Bard Theatre.

I knew what I had to do.

It turned out that theatre people start their day a lot later than stable boys and flower sellers.

It was ten o'clock in the morning before anyone opened the doors at the Bard. It was noon when a thin grey gelding pulling a hired hansom stopped at the stage door.

"Thank you." A woman in a dark blue cape with the hood pulled over her head stepped out.

It was her. I did not need to see her face to know.

She paid the driver and turned towards the theatre.

"Mother!" I cried. She did not stop. Perhaps she had not heard me. Maybe it was the noise. A wagoner was unloading barrels of beer across the street.

"Mother!" I cried again.

She stepped through the stage door.

"Mother!" This isn't how I'd meant our meeting to be at all. I was shrieking like a fishwife. But the door was swinging closed, so I called out: "Miss Valentina Green. . ."

"My dear!" She turned towards me at last. Her hood fell back as she swung around. Her hair tumbled down over her shoulders – coppery-gold without her Cleopatra wig, just like the picture in the nursery. Our eyes met. Hers were emerald green – far brighter than even her portrait or the poster had promised they would be.

She held my gaze and my heart thumped like a galloping horse.

"H-hello," I whispered. "I came to see you, I–I hope you don't mind. . ."

"Of course not." Her voice was rich and warm. She held up her slender gloved hand before I could say another word. She smiled so kindly, I thought that I would melt like snow.

"It is very good of you to wait for me in the cold," she went on. "But if you want me to sign autographs, you will have to return again after the show."

"But—but I don't want an autograph," I said, talking fast before I could lose my nerve. "It's me. Your daughter. Josie . . . Josephine."

She took a step back and seemed to see me properly for the first time. She gave a little cry of amazement. "You? Can it really be?"

"Yes." I blushed as those emerald eyes looked me up and down again. "I am Josephine, your daughter."

"Good lord!" She gasped. "What a ghastly hat!"

If Mother was shocked by Doris's hat, she screamed when she saw my hair.

I cannot blame her really. She is so pretty herself. And she is used to such fine things.

We were sitting in her dressing room amongst her jewels and furs by then, and I was telling her the whole story of how I had run away from Summer's Place.

I had to tell her first that Father was dead, of course. My voice cracked and two tears like perfect pearls ran down her pale cheek.

"Poor man. Poor foolish Charles," she said. Then

she dabbed her eyes with a white lace handkerchief and stared into the huge looking glass above her dressing table. "Carry on, do carry on. . ."

I was just telling her about Black Beauty when Mother sprang to her feet.

"Neville. Neville!" she called.

A chubby man, dressed in a lettuce-green velvet suit with a gold cravat, squeezed through the door. I learned later he was Mother's theatre manager.

"What is it, cherub?" he asked.

"Do you think I should wear mourning, Neville? I have just learned I am a widow," she said.

"Mourning?" The plump man opened and closed his mouth like a toad catching flies. "Certainly not. It's so very. . ." Neville seemed lost for words. Perhaps he was just sad to hear Mother's news that her husband had died. "It's so very. . ."

"Black?" said Mother.

"Well quite." Neville squeezed back out of the door and Mother began to brush her golden-red hair.

"He's right, of course," she said. "Black clothes can make the skin look so dull. . . Do carry on with your story, darling."

I did the best I could. Making her laugh with my impressions of Doris and Daisy in the laundry and even striding up and down the dressing room to show her how I had learned to walk like a boy.

"Bravo!" She clapped her hands. "Maybe we should use you as a little page in *Anthony and Cleopatra*. Neville would love that... Neville?" She summoned the manager again.

"Oh no! I should hate it. And anyway," I said, firmly as Neville reached the door, "I can't be in a play. I have to be outside. I have to find Black Beauty."

"Horses, horses, horses! You are just like your father!" Mother threw down her hairbrush.

"Is that such a bad thing?" I bit my lip.

Mother saw at once that I was sad. Although she didn't turn around – she was pinning up her hair – she smiled at me in the looking glass and her eyes lit up with such warmth that I felt better again at once.

"I'm sorry, darling. You must forgive me. Only, it's all so new," she said. "It's like I've been cast in a fresh role and I must learn how to play the part. I must learn how to be your mother."

"Ha! It might just be your greatest performance yet!" said Neville, hovering in the doorway.

Something about the way he said it sounded

unkind. But I must have been wrong, because Mother seemed delighted.

"Do you really think so?" She leapt to her feet and did what I had been waiting for her to do for so long. She gathered me into her arms and gave me a hug.

She smelt of lilies and violets and expensive perfumes which probably came all the way from Paris and...

Oh no! I thought with horror how I must smell of turnip and old cabbages from sleeping in the market. I hadn't washed once since I came to London.

"Now, Josephine, my darling daughter," said Mother, stepping back and wrinkling her nose a little, "I have made a plan. When this play is over, I am going to give up the stage for good. We will sell my jewels." She picked up a string of rubies and pearls from the table. "If you have found your horse by then, I will buy him from the cab driver and we'll move to the country. We'll get a little cottage with honeysuckle and roses around the door..."

"Sensational, my dear!" Neville clapped his hands.

"Oh Mama!" I flung my arms around her neck. I didn't care if I did smell of cabbages. "Do you really mean it? You, me and Black Beauty? In the country?

That will be perfect," I said. I could hardly believe it; not an hour ago I had been shivering in the streets, and now I was safe and warm and loved. And, finally, I had a real chance of getting Beauty back – if only I could find him.

Chapter Thirty-nine

The Bard Theatre was like a beehive – always busy. Actors and actresses buzzed about backstage, singing and practising dance steps or rehearsing their lines. The young women were often wearing almost nothing but their underwear as they dashed down the narrow corridors to costume fittings, their faces powdered and their lips and cheeks bright red with rouge. Meanwhile the stagehands whistled and cursed as they painted scenery or hung huge lamps to light the stage.

Then, just moments before each show, a strange calm would descend, everyone would step into their places and the magic of the performance would begin.

Exciting as it all was, life in the theatre was not

quite as I expected. For one thing, I never did get to see as much of Mother as I hoped. She was the star of the show – always on stage or in rehearsals. And she hardly ever came into theatre until the afternoon. She had to go out to lunch with gentlemen a lot. Dinner too.

"It is all part of being an actress," she explained. "Although it really is impossible to keep slim when one must eat out every day!"

We did not live together either as I'd hoped we would.

Mother explained about that too.

"My apartment is tiny. Just a little bird's nest really. And an actress must – well, I must – entertain gentlemen sometimes after dinner and... Well, Josephine, my darling, I am sure you understand. Daughters and admirers do not always go together."

I didn't understand. Not really.

"You can sleep in my dressing room," Mother had said on my first evening. "It'll be such fun. You can you use my Egyptian cotton shawl as a blanket, and doze on the chaise longue pretending you are in Paris."

The chaise longue turned out to be a narrow, lumpy daybed with little gold buttons that dug into my back. But at least it was more comfy than the hard ground underneath the old fruit and vegetable wagons and the dressing room was warm and snug.

Sometimes, when I was all alone at night, I would dress up in Mother's scarves and hats, clip her earrings on and wear her strings of pearls around my neck.

I stared into the looking glass for hours, pretending I was her.

In the daytime, I wasn't allowed in the dressing room – especially not before a performance. I had to keep out of the way as much as possible. That suited me. I wanted to be out, looking for Beauty. I followed every rumour and every lead. Mac had heard of a cab man in Kilburn with a black horse with a white star, and Arthur the usher had seen one in the streets once or twice, whose owner called him "Jack".

At the end of my first month at the Bard, I was just dashing out of the door, setting off on my usual round searching the Covent Garden streets, when Neville called me back.

"Time you earned your keep, Josephine Green," he said. "You're sleeping in my theatre. If you still refuse to appear on stage, you can carry this with you instead." He waddled towards me with two enormous boards tied together at the top like a bib. There was a picture of Mother's face on each side.

Miss Valentina Green
at The Bard Theatre, Drury Lane.
Seats, Boxes & Standing Room Available.

I had seen men carrying advertisements around on "sandwich" boards like this many times. Every street urchin in Covent Garden thought it was funny to throw mud at them and see it stick against the boards at the back. They liked to spin the men around and send them wobbling into the road like spinning tops. Once in the road, the cab drivers and coachmen shouted "out of the way!" and hit the poor boardmen with their whips.

"Is there a problem?" Neville was standing so close I could smell his hot, liquorice-y breath.

"No," I said. "No problem."

The minute I stepped on to Drury Lane, a gaggle of street boys went wild.

"It's a girl! It's a girl! It's a girl boardman!" they

cried and they chased me all down Bow Street, throwing mud and rotten fruit and stones.

Mother was furious when she saw me later.

"There's a tomato in her hair, for goodness' sake, Neville. How dare you send Josephine out like that? I forbid you to ever..."

"It's all right!" I said. "I like it." That wasn't true exactly; the board was heavy, it was hard work trudging the streets, and I frequently had to dodge rotten fruit. But towards the end of the day I had made friends with the other boardmen, and I quickly realized this gave me eyes all over London.

"Keep a look out while you're walking," I begged them. "If you ever see a black cab horse, with a white star on his head, let me know."

"You are a peculiar girl. Sometimes, I don't understand you at all, Josephine," sighed Mother. "You are prepared to make a spectacle of yourself walking up and down like a human signpost, but you won't even step on the stage." She hurried off to be fitted for a pair of snow white leather boots. "At least it keeps you busy," she called over her shoulder. "... Just until we move to the country, my darling."

She didn't try and stop me carrying the boards again.

One day early in the new year, I had a brilliant idea.

"I am going to stick Beauty's picture to the board on my back," I explained to Arthur when I stopped outside the opera house on my morning route. "Think how many people will know I am searching for him then!"

I wasn't any good at drawing myself, but I described Beauty carefully to Ivan, a boy who painted scenery at the Bard. He drew a wonderful likeness of him and we wrote underneath it in thick red paint:

MISSING HORSE. BELIEVED TO BE PULLING A CAB. PLEASE LEAVE WORD AT THE BARD THEATRE IF SEEN.

Arthur looked after the picture for me at the opera house. He stuck it on my back each morning and took it off again each night. Neville would be furious if he knew I was covering his advertisements with an image of Black Beauty, but I was getting desperate. All the leads we'd had so far had run dry. The horse in Kilburn turned out not to be black at all. Just dark grey. And Arthur never saw the mysterious "Jack" trotting by with his cab again.

*

Spring came and there were daffodils in the flower market, great banks of bright yellow like streaming sun.

"Still no luck with your beloved Black Diamond?" asked Mother one morning a few weeks after Valentine's Day.

"His name's Black Beauty," I said, a little crossly. "And no! I still haven't found him." I was fighting not to lose hope. It had been so long now.

"Good!" said Mother, brightly. "I mean, not good that you haven't found him; I'm just pleased that you are not ready to move to the countryside ... quite yet. You see Neville's putting on *A Midsummer Night's Dream* next and he simply can't find anybody else to play Titania the Fairy Queen."

"Of course," I said. And when the play opened at Easter, Mother was truly wonderful in the part. I had seen all her different roles, but she looked most beautiful as the jealous Fairy Queen. Her hair was loose. She wore a pink satin gown with rosebud slippers and gossamer wings. She flew above the audience on strings as thin as silk and everybody gasped. Each time I saw Mother on the stage, the more I understood how impossible it must have been for her to be hidden away living the life of a country lady, with horses and dogs for company.

All London seemed to burst with life as the weather turned bright and warm. No longer huddled in their cloaks, theatregoers paraded up and down the streets in all their finery. Before the lights dimmed for the show each night, the rows of seats looked like a rainbow, the ladies wore so many different colours of satin and silk. Even the gentlemen wore bright cravats and waistcoats. The flower market looked more and more beautiful too. Like a meadow, just as Mac had promised.

As well as daffodils, there were tulips and crocuses, blue hyacinths and lily-of-the-valley.

"Buy a posy," called the flower sellers. "Buy a posy for your love!"

"What about you, Josie-of-the-boards?" teased Old Meg who had a pitch selling violets on the corner of Floral Street. All the sellers knew me by now. "Don't you have no one to buy flowers for?"

Meg meant I should buy flowers for a sweetheart but I didn't have one. And, now it was spring again, all I could think about was Father. He had been dead for over a year. If only I could lay a posy on his grave. He had always loved wild flowers, pointing them out to me as I rode Merrylegs beside him down the lanes.

"No." I shook my head. "I have no one, Meg," I said.

I turned to step off the kerb, and narrowly missed being struck as a cab rattled past, the horse's hooves thundering. "Look out!" Meg grabbed my arm. "What is it, Josie?" she said. "You look like you've seen a ghost?"

"I think I have!" I slipped out of the board and let it clatter to the ground. "Look after that for me," I cried, as I broke into a run. "I recognize that poor cab horse."

Chapter Forty

The cab had stopped outside the opera house and I ran breathlessly up to the horse. I was right. I did recognize her.

It was Ginger.

"Ginger?" I cried. "Can that really be you?" Her bright chestnut coat was as dull as rust, her legs were bowed and her breathing rasped like a creaky door in the wind. But I knew it was her. Her ears were laid flat against her head – just as they always had been when she first came to Birtwick, before James and Mr Manly showed her kindness.

"Ginger?" She lifted her long thin neck and her ears pricked as I called her name. Lady Magpie's son, George, must have ridden her flat out until she was broken – just as he had done with Linnet and so many other horses who had been ruined by the cruelty of life at Earlshall. I tried not to think about Beauty and his shattered knees. I tried not to imagine him looking like Ginger.

"It's me, Ginger, old girl," I said, slipping my hand under her bridle, and rubbing the side of her tired face. "It's Joe Green, do you remember?"

Ginger sighed and let the weight of her head fall against me. I wasn't sure if she did remember or if it was just exhaustion.

"It's all right," I whispered. "It's going to be all right."

"Oy! What are you doing?" cried the driver, cracking his whip at me as two fat gentlemen climbed into the cab. It rocked and groaned as they slammed the door and Ginger shivered under the weight.

"Get out of the way," ordered the cabby. "You are holding up my fare."

"No!" I said. "This horse can't go anywhere. Don't you see? She's tired to death."

Lines of old dry sweat were caked into her coat and it didn't look as if she'd had a square meal for weeks. As her sides heaved, her ribs stuck out like the bones of a corset.

"Hurry up, driver." One of the fat red-faced gentleman stuck his head out of the window.

"We have a lunch in Piccadilly," hollered his friend.

"No!" I said again as the edge of the driver's whip caught my shoulder. I thought of Mother's jewels and how she had promised to buy Beauty. Well, there were so many jewels ... surely we could buy two horses. "Wait!" I said, as the driver raised his arm to crack his whip again. "I'll buy this horse from you. I'll buy Ginger."

"Ginger?" spat the driver. "This is Lady."

"That nag? A lady?" The red-faced man laughed.

"She is Ginger," I said to the driver. "And I'll buy her off you for ten pounds. . ."

"Ten pounds? You're having a laugh." The driver sniggered. "She's not mine to sell anyway. I only hire her by the day."

"Twenty pounds, then," I said. "Surely your bosses wouldn't argue with that?"

"Er. . ." The driver rubbed his eyes in confusion. "Twenty pounds?" he muttered. I saw a bead of sweat drip down his long thin nose.

"I've had enough of this!" growled the red-faced passenger. Another cab had pulled up behind us and the two fat gentlemen opened the door and began to squeeze out. "We'll get someone else to take us, if you're going to stand here bartering all day."

"Wait," said the driver. "I'll take you."

"Thirty," I said and the driver shook my hand as the two fat men waddled away and took the cab behind us.

"See!" I kissed Ginger on the nose. "Didn't I tell you it would be all right? You're saved. All we need to do is find Mother and get the money to pay for you."

"Wait here!" I told the cabby as Ginger stumbled to a stop outside the Bard.

"Thirty pounds, remember," he said, rubbing his hands together. I was sure he would tell the cab company he sold Ginger for twenty and keep the difference, but I didn't care. Just so long as I could set her free.

"Don't go anywhere!" I dashed in to the theatre and ran towards the dressing rooms downstairs. "Mother," I called. "Mother, I need thirty pounds."

"Thirty pounds?" She was lying on the chaise longue nibbling turkish delight but sat up like a jack-in-the-box as I burst in. "Thirty pounds? Whatever do you need with that kind of money, darling?"

"I need to buy a horse. . ."

"Your horse?" She looked surprised and a little flustered. "You found him?"

"No, it's not Beauty I've found. It's Ginger. She was Beauty's friend. She was special to James – He was my friend and. . .

"Darling. Darling. Darling. Slow down!" Mother raised her thin white hand to her brow as if she had a headache. "Let me get this straight; you want to buy a horse who is a friend of your horse and you want thirty pounds to do it?"

"Yes, please," I said, grinning with the warm joy that was growing inside me. Ginger was in a terrible state, but we could help her. "She needs rest and plenty of grass," I explained. "She's dreadfully thin. And she can barely breathe. Her wind must be damaged. Her legs are swollen badly, but if we can take her to the country. . ."

"I do not have thirty pounds," said Mother.

"But. . ." For a moment I was confused. Then I saw what she meant. "Oh. You don't have thirty pounds in cash." I was thinking fast. "Well that's all right; we can explain to the driver about your jewellery. We can tell him you've just got to sell something and then. . ."

"Oh, Josephine darling." She sank back on to the couch. "I cannot sell my jewellery." Her voice sounded cold and flat.

"Please, Mother," I begged. "The money's not for me. It's for Ginger. . ."

"Stop! I cannot sell my jewellery because it is not worth anything." She stretched to the dressing table and grabbed a string of pearls. "Paste." She let them fall into her lap and lifted a gold bracelet. "Painted tin! See?"

"And the rubies?" I asked, a thick foggy sickness rising in my throat.

"Just red glass," said Mother with a sigh. "It's costume jewellery. All of it. I wore the pearls to play Desdemona. The rubies were for Lady Macbeth. This" – she picked up the thick gold bracelet again – "this was for Cleopatra. Surely you realized that?"

"Like the black wig?" I had been an idiot. It was all just pretend. "But I don't understand," I said slowly. "You said you could rescue Beauty. You said we could buy a country cottage. I thought you were rich?"

"Well, I'm not." She folded her arms. "Honestly, Josephine. All this country cottage and everything. Finding Black Diamond. . ."

"Beauty. His name is Black Beauty!" How is it she could learn a hundred lines in a day but she couldn't learn that?

"Yes, Black Beauty," she said, with a wave of her hand. "Well, we might have to delay that a little. You see, now is a very difficult time for me." Tears were filling her eyes. "I want Neville to cast me in his next play, *Romeo and Juliet*. And people are so cruel, darling. They are saying that I am too old to play Juliet."

I swallowed hard. Trying to breathe.

"Excuse me?" Ivan the set painter was standing nervously in the doorway. "There's a cab man outside, waiting with a horse. He wants to know if you are you going to buy her or not?"

"No." I buried my head in my hands. Poor Ginger. I had promised to save her and I couldn't. "Tell the cab man we cannot buy her after all," I whispered. "Tell him we have no money."

I saw Ginger again, one last time.

It was late in the evening, about a week later. I was walking across Trafalgar Square with my board when, as I reached St Martin's church, a big flat cart rattled past. I glanced up and saw that a horse was lying on the back, half covered with a piece of ragged sack. I think I knew it would be Ginger even before I could force myself to turn my head and see for sure.

She raised her neck a little and tried to look at me. But the effort was too much. Her head fell back.

"Don't," I said, leaping down from the kerb as the cart stopped in traffic. "Don't try to move, Ginger, old girl. I'm here."

She sighed gently as I stroked the long streak of white fur which ran from her forelock to her chestnut nose. I thought of how often James had stroked that same white blaze. "Like a splash of spilt milk," he used to say.

"You remember James, don't you?" I whispered. Ginger sighed again – a long, deep rattling sigh. Then her big brown eyes flickered closed. "Shh!" I laid my hand on her cheek. "Just rest now."

The cart moved off and I watched it weave through the traffic. I did not try to chase after it. There was no point. Ginger was dead.

Perhaps, as she had slipped away, she remembered Birtwick, the only place she had ever been happy. Perhaps Ginger imagined she was galloping over the common; one last ride with James on her back, racing with Beauty and me.

"Goodbye," I murmured as the cart disappeared around the corner at last. "At least you're at peace now, Ginger."

And the bells of St Martin's church began to ring.

Chapter
Forty-one

After Ginger, I stopped searching the streets for Beauty. There was little point now. Even if I found him, I would only let him down, just like I had let Ginger down.

Mother and I mostly kept out of each other's way. Now the promise of the country cottage was shattered, we didn't seem to have much to say.

She was busy, anyway. She had convinced Neville she would make a wonderful Juliet. And she was right.

I watched rehearsals, hidden in the back row of the stalls, as she skipped and laughed and threw her head back, making herself seem like a young girl no older than Doris. Only a year or two older than me . . . certainly not old enough to have a grown daughter of her own. She was beautiful, her bronze hair tied back in a simple plait. She glowed with the happiness she always had when she began a new part.

The night the play opened, I watched her steal the show. She wore a sky-blue dress and a "diamond" tiara made of sparkling glass. People's heads turned as she moved across the stage. Grown men wept when she was buried with her Romeo and the audience rose to their feet and cheered for her at the end.

"Your greatest performance ever, my dear Valentina," cried Neville.

But for me, although Mother's part was beautiful and romantic and sad, it was the nursemaid who moved me most. When young Juliet was in trouble it was never her mother, Lady Capulet, who helped her; it was always the rosy-cheeked nurse. As I watched I could only think of one person.

"Nanny Clay," I whispered and, while everyone was laughing at the funny old nurse, I burst into tears. Suddenly I wanted the person who had always cared for me the most. I wanted her desperately.

"Mother, I need to talk to you," I said, next morning.

"Not now, darling. I have four gentlemen to see me in the lobby. The papers are saying my performance was sensational, you know."

"It was. You were brilliant," I said, and reached up to kiss her. It was true; she was a wonderful actress, but I realized she had only ever been playing the part of mother to me. "Good luck. And . . . goodbye."

"What a funny little thing you are, darling," she said, tucking a curl behind my ear. My hair had grown almost to my shoulders again. "I'll see you later." Then she kissed the top of my head and hurried away.

When I slipped out of the Bard Theatre half an hour afterwards, I left a note behind a string of pearls on her looking glass. I knew she would understand. It was a little bit like the note she had left for Father once.

Darling Mother,

I am leaving London. I love you and I will miss you but I know the theatre is the only life that makes you happy. I would never want to take that away from you. Do not look for me. Perhaps I will find a country cottage of my own.

Your dearest daughter,

Josephine.

Then I walked towards Charing Cross, where I knew Mac was often waiting with Pinky and the cab. Sure enough I found him on the corner and waved. His big face lit up with a broad grin.

"Found that horse of yours yet, lassie?"

"No – and I realize now that I never shall," I said. "I am done with London."

Mac nodded. He did not try to change my mind. Perhaps he had feared my search was hopeless all along.

"Do you know where the village of Fairstowe is?" I asked him. "I need to get there. I want to find my old nanny."

I had always remembered the name of the place where Nanny Clay told me she was going to live with her nephew when Aunt Lavinia sent her away. It sounded so pretty. I hoped she would be waiting for me.

Mac listened attentively as I told him of my plan, and then looked at a scruffy road map he kept rolled up under his seat.

"You might just be in luck, lass," he said with a whistle. He said he knew a cabby who was driving to a town not far from Fairstowe that very day.

"Your nanny may have moved on since," Mac warned me gently. "It's been some time."

"I'll take my chance," I said.

"I'm sure Ben will give you a ride," said Mac. "The town he's going to is about ten miles on past Fairstowe. There's a fellow there buys and sells old cab horses. Ben's grey mare isn't as strong as she was; he wants to go down and have a look for something new."

I closed my ears. I didn't want to listen to any more talk of tired old cab horses. So long as Ben was going to Fairstowe, that was good enough for me.

"Thank you, Mac," I said, hugging him until he blushed as bright as Pinky's coat. "Thank you for everything you've done for me."

Mac's friend Ben was a small, jolly man and, although his grey mare was old and slow, the journey passed swiftly enough. It was a glorious spring day and we soon left London behind and were trotting along country lanes, with white cow parsley in the hedges and daisies along the side of the grassy verge. Ben told funny stories about growing up far away from London with wild black ponies in the Yorkshire dales.

We stopped near a stream and ate bread and ham for our lunch, then drove on for another hour until we reached the edge of a pretty village with no more than seven or eight houses, a big thatched-roof farm and a pub.

"Here you are. Fairstowe! Is this the place?" asked Ben.

"I hope so," I said.

"I wish I could stay and see you settled," said Ben. "But if I'm going to get to this horse dealer in Newton, and be back to London by night..."

"Go," I said, "I'll be fine."

As Ben trotted away I saw a farmer with a black-and-white collie dog opening a gate on to the lane. Perhaps he would know something about Nanny Clay's nephew.

"Excuse me," I called. "Is there a young man who lives near here called Clay?"

"Nathan Clay? First cottage on the left. Chickens in the garden. You can't miss it," said the farmer.

I knocked on the door and it was opened by a young man wearing a cloth cap and a farmhand's smock. I could hear a baby crying in the background.

"My Auntie Joan did come," he said. "But she didn't stay. We had little enough room to begin with, and with the baby..."

"Oh!" My heart sank like a stone in a well. "So Nanny Clay's gone?" I said.

"Not far! Don't look so worried," said Nathan. "She's up there at Hexham Hall. Big house. On the hill." He stepped out on to the path and pointed over the fields.

I saw a grand white house with a sweeping driveway between a row of trees and lush green parkland stretching out on every side.

"Hexham Hall?" I knew that name. "Not Lady Hexham?" I said, remembering the old lady who Aunt Lavinia had tried to send me away to be companion to.

"That's the one." Nathan nodded.

"Lady Hexham who never goes out? The recluse?" I asked.

"Recluse? Not any more!" Nathan chuckled. "Not since Auntie got her hands on her. They're opening up the house, having guests to tea and all sorts now!"

I laughed. "Good old Nanny Clay." I should have guessed. No one would be allowed to shut themselves away while she was in charge.

"Well, bless me," said Nathan, looking at me hard. "You must be Miss Josephine." He smiled politely and took off his cap. "Auntie spoke of you so often."

"Yes – I am Miss Josephine." I was wearing a pretty green dress that had been made for one of the fairies in *A Midsummer Night's Dream* and my short hair was tucked behind a neat Alice band of emerald ribbon. Perhaps, I did look a bit like the young lady of the manor again, the girl Nanny Clay used to know. She would never have believed it if she had seen me as Joe Green the stable lad.

"You get on up to that house as fast as you can, miss," said Nathan with a smile. "Old Auntie Joan will burst with joy to see you again."

"Thank you! I will. . ." And I began to run along the lane, over the fields and up the sunny slope towards the big white house on top of the hill.

Part Six
Hexham Hall

Chapter Forty-two

As soon as Nanny Clay put her arms around me, I remembered the scent of her lavender soap. I remembered the comfort of those broad shoulders. But I had forgotten how wide her big blue eyes grew when she was shocked. And she *was* shocked ... plenty of times, as I told my tale, up in the little nursery at the top of the grand white house. If the walls had been yellow instead of cream, I might have believed us home again in Summer's Place.

"You slept in a stable? Oh, Josie."

And she cried and hugged me so tight I could barely breathe when I told her how James and I had rescued the horses and escaped from the fire.

When I told her about my time with Mother she

said nothing but cleared her throat and sighed a lot.

"I don't blame her," I said. "She tried her best to be a good mother. But she loves theatre with such passion... I know how it feels to care about something so much, I really do."

Nanny Clay cleared her throat and sighed again. "As long as you've come to understand her. That's all that matters," she said. "I know you love her. She is your mother."

I wanted to tell Nanny Clay that *she* was my mother too. I wanted to tell her how I felt when I saw Lady Capulet and the Nurse in *Romeo and Juliet*. But I knew she would only be embarrassed. Instead, I let her gather me into a hug and laid my head on her shoulder. "I love you, Nanny Clay."

"I love you too, pet. And I'm sorry you never found your horse," she said. "I am sorry about poor Black Beauty. He must have been very special..."

"Thank you," I whispered. I had forgotten how it is to be with someone who listens to every word you say, and understands things which are not even spoken out loud. It was as if Nanny Clay had looked inside me and seen my heart was broken into a thousand tiny pieces. She did not try to make me feel better. She did not tell me I was silly – that Black Beauty was only a horse. She just let me talk and, as I talked, she tried to understand.

"Well, pet," she said when it was dark outside at last and I had almost talked myself hoarse, "we had better introduce you to Lady Hexham. We must convince her to let you stay. But Lord knows how you will make yourself useful to her."

"I think I might have an idea about that," I said with a grin.

"Good gracious, Josie." Nanny Clay's eyes grew wide with worry. "Whatever are you planning now?"

"You want to be my stable lad?" Lady Hexham was a big woman, who looked a little like a sad walrus. But she peered at me with her small bright eyes and smiled. "All right, Josephine. Why not?"

"I will tell you why not, Your Ladyship," said Nanny Clay firmly. "First of all, Josie is the daughter of Sir Charles Green ... and secondly ... well, as you can see, madam, she is a girl."

Lady Hexham nodded her big grey head. "She is the daughter of a baronet; but unless she is too proud to work..."

"I am not too proud," I said quickly. "I love

working in stables. I want to be around horses for the rest of my life."

"Good." Lady Hexham smiled again. "That's settled. I shall need someone to open up the stables." She leant forward. "My goddaughter, Miss Ellen Blomefield, is an orphan and I am her guardian. I neglected her when ... well, when I could not face the world and shut myself away. But now I have invited her to live here at Hexham. Ellen is seventeen and very pretty. I am sure that she will want to hold parties and gallavant around the countryside in a carriage. We will fill the stables for her ... and for the young men who'll come to visit. After all, she is to inherit my fortune and will be quite a catch."

Lady Hexham laughed so much she began to wheeze.

"But that's wonderful," I said, beginning to pace up and down the drawing room, my head bursting with ideas. "There is a good hay loft, a carriage shed and plenty of fine stalls – a little white wash and it will look as good as new in no time. Then there are the horses you will need..."

"First, something sensible to pull a little trap for me," said Lady Hexham. "Nothing too fancy. But if I am to go out and about in the world, as your dear old Nanny Clay insists I must, then I shall begin by taking a turn around the country lanes. As I remember, they are very pretty at this time of year."

"Oh, they are!" I said. "We shall find you the perfect horse, a true gentleman. . ." My voice caught in my throat for a moment; I couldn't help thinking about poor Beauty. But I took a deep breath and carried on. "There's a bank of honeysuckle just before Fairstowe village that you can smell from the top of the hill. And the woods will be full of bluebells in a week or two."

"This is all very well," said Nanny Clay firmly. "But the problem still remains. Josie cannot be a stable lad. She is a girl! She cannot go back to chopping off her hair and binding her bosoms and all that nonsense." She folded her arms over her own enormous chest. "It just won't do."

"You are right, as always," said Lady Hexham. "Josephine cannot be a stable lad."

"No! That's not fair," I cried. "Please! I can do the job as well as any boy. I promise you, I can."

Lady Hexham held up her podgy pink hand.

"If you cannot be a stable lad, you will just have to be a stable girl," she said, wheezing with laughter and she smiled at Nanny Clay. "It is 1877, you know.

We've had a queen on the throne for forty years . . . the country seems to be doing fine under the rule of a woman; I am sure my stables can cope with a girl for a groom."

"Thank you!" I fell to my knees and kissed Lady Hexham's hand as if she was Queen Victoria herself.

"Honestly!" said Nanny Clay. But she was laughing too.

As we left the drawing room, Lady Hexham rang a little silver bell.

"Ah, Wilson," she said as her butler appeared. "Send word to the dealer in Newton. Tell him to bring something quiet for Josephine to look at. She is to be my new groom, you know."

"Your . . . your groom?" Poor Wilson looked as if he had swallowed a fly. "Very good, my lady," he said as he gathered himself together.

That night as I snuggled down in the nursery, my head was whirling with schemes and plans for the new stables, wondering what sort of horse the dealer from Newton would bring.

Chapter
Forty-three

I was round the back of the stable block, by the muck heap, whitewashing a wall when the dealer came. He wasn't due until two o'clock but he came early and took me by surprise.

"Hello," he called picking his way across the bumpy ground. "You must be the new stable lad, I mean groom. I mean ... oh dear." He looked me up and down in confusion. I was wearing a pair of baggy corduroy trousers I had borrowed from the gardener, a white shirt tucked in at the waist and a big red-and-white spotty handkerchief tied around my hair.

"Pleased to meet you," I said, wiping my hand and leaning down from the ladder. "I'm Josie, and you are quite right, I am Lady Hexham's new groom."

"William Thoroughgood, pleased to meet you too, miss." He smiled in a way that seemed friendly, even if he was surprised. "I left the horse tied up in the yard," he said. "We're ready when you are."

"Do you mind if I just finish this patch, while I'm up the ladder?" I said, pointing to a last square of wall which needed whitewash before I was done.

"Go ahead," said Mr Thoroughgood, leaning against the fence behind him and watching me work. He had probably never seen a girl paint a wall before. "You carry on, miss. Old Jack won't mind waiting a minute or two in the sunshine."

"Jack?" I asked, pausing before dipping my brush into the whitewash.

I remembered how Arthur had seen a black cab horse passing the opera house once or twice. He said the cabby had called him Jack. I dipped my brush again and saw that my hand was shaking. It was silly. It wouldn't be Beauty. It couldn't be. I tried to stop the little flame of hope that was leaping in my chest.

"I hear you get horses from London sometimes?" I said, trying to keep my voice steady. "Is that where you found Jack?"

"Jack? No." Mr Thoroughgood shook his head.

The flame snuffed out. Of course it wasn't him.

There must be a million horses known as Jack. Still –

"What colour is he?" I asked.

"Black," said Mr Thoroughgood. "Nice-looking horse. Or would have been once. That's why I thought he might suit Lady H—"

"Black?" The foolish flame flickered inside me again.

"Dark as midnight," said Mr Thoroughgood. "I picked him up at a fair the other side of Newton from a corn dealer. Now you mention it, he did come from London before then. He was a cab horse they say, well-looked after before his owner got sick." He grinned. "Although I'll bet he didn't pull a cab all his life. Not this one."

"No?" I was gripping the ladder tightly with both hands. My knees were shaking. If I moved an inch, I would fall.

"You all right up there, missy?" said Mr Thoroughgood.

Before I could answer I heard a high-pitched whinny from the stable yard.

"Beauty!" I cried, leaping from the ladder and sending the pot of whitewash flying as I ran.

"Beauty? Now that would be a good name for him," Mr Thoroughgood called after me. "He's got a. . ."

"A star in the middle of his forehead. I know," I shouted as I skidded around the corner. And there he was. My beloved, beautiful horse, standing in the yard. We looked into each others' eyes and neither of us moved for a moment. It was really him. I felt if I blinked he might vanish and I'd find the whole thing had been a dream. Then he threw his head in the air and whinnied with delight. I dashed forward and flung my arms around his neck.

"It's you!" I said, as he nuzzled my ear. "I promised I would find you, Black Beauty. But you found me ... you did it, Beauty. I should have known you would."

When I stopped hugging Beauty at last, I looked up and Mr Thoroughgood smiled.

"You two know each other then?" he said.

"Yes." I wiped the tears from my eyes. Grooms probably aren't meant to cry. "We are dear friends." Although, now I looked at Beauty, I could see he was very different from the fine horse I had known. Earlshall and London had taken their toll. His coat was dull and he was dreadfully thin.

"And your poor knees," I said, sinking to the ground and running my fingers over the scars.

"He's battered but not broken," said Mr Thoroughgood. "Lots of grass and plenty of rest and he'll make a fine horse again."

"And love too," I whispered in Beauty's ear as

I led him to a stall. "We'll buy him from you, Mr Thoroughgood, whatever price you ask. He is just what we want."

Beauty soon grew fat on summer grass and I groomed him every day until his coat shone like polished ebony again.

"What a beauty he is, indeed," said Lady Hexham when I walked him up to the front of the house for her to admire.

And we started to go as far as the village and back in the trap most days. Beauty was as quiet as a lamb, of course, but his ears were pricked and I could feel his old spirit coming back.

When the repairs in the yard were finished, I brought a useful cob and a pair of bay carriage horses from Mr Thoroughgood too.

"You're doing a grand job, these old stables are coming back to life," he said, looking around and nodding. I felt a warm glow of pride.

And when Miss Ellen, Lady Hexham's goddaughter came, we found her a side-saddle mare and a spare hunter for her gentleman friends. She was a laughing, happy girl, who was gentle with the horses and kind to me.

"This is all splendid, Josie," said Lady Hexham as I drove her past the woods full of bluebells one sunny evening. "You are proving a fine stable girl. But it's too much work for you on your own, I think. We should get a coachman too."

"I know just the person for the job," I said.

And I wrote to James at Earlshall, begging him to come.

I kept the letter simple. There were so many things he did not know. Things I would need to tell him face to face. That poor Ginger was dead. That I was a girl.

I wrote only:

Dear James,
Please come to Hexham Hall. It is a fine place and there is a job as coachman if you want it.
Beauty is here too.
Your dear friend,
J –

What should I write? How should I sign my name?

Your dear friend,
J. Green.

He would see the truth for himself soon enough.

Nanny Clay made me write another letter too.

"You must tell your aunt and cousin what has become of you," she said.

"Why? They don't care," I objected.

"It is proper, that's why," said Nanny Clay. "And your dear father and I raised you to know what is right."

I couldn't argue with that. So I wrote:

Dear Aunt Lavinia and Cousin Eustace,

I have arrived with Lady Hexham at last. She is most kind, but I am not her companion as you had planned. I am her stable girl. It is a job which I love. You always did say I was fit for nothing but horses and hay.

Yours dutifully,
Josephine.

No one from Summer's Place ever wrote back. But I like to think of Aunt Lavinia and The Slug looking shocked as they read my letter at breakfast one morning. Perhaps Eustace almost choked on his boiled egg!

It was a long time until I heard from James and

I started to wonder if I ever would. We had a letter from Mr York the coachman, who wrote to say that James had left Earlshall without a reference; Lady Magpie had refused to give him one. But Mr York said he had forwarded my letter to a livery yard where he heard James was working early in the summer.

At last the reply I had been waiting for came.

I will be with you on Tuesday.
    Your grateful friend,
    James Howard

All morning I paced up and down in the stables, stopping to stroke Beauty every time I passed.

Then, silently as a shadow, James was there, behind me in the yard.

"Hello!" As I spun round, the smile dropped from his lips and he raised his eyebrows and stood staring at me. "Why – why you're. . ."

"A girl," I said, talking so fast my words fell over each other. "I'm sorry, James. I should have told you." I was wearing the gardener's corduroy trousers again, with the red-and-white handkerchief tied around my hair. "It's just. . ."

"No." James shook his head. "It's not that. You're..."

"A groom," I said, pointing to the stables. "I know! Imagine me, being in charge of all this..."

"No," said James, a red blush creeping up his cheeks. "It's not that either. You're..."

"What?" I cried. "What am I, James?"

"You're beautiful," he said.

"Oh." Now my cheeks were burning too.

Then, thankfully, Beauty whinnied and we both began to talk about the horses as fast as we could.

Later, when we led Beauty out to the paddock to graze, we leant against the gate and I told James about Ginger and how I had last seen her carried away on that dreadful cart. I told him too how I had bought a posy of fresh violets from Meg and laid them on the spot outside the church where Ginger had passed by.

His eyes filled with tears. He turned away and bit his lip. Then he kicked the bottom of the gate.

"Damn them at Earlshall. Damn them all," he said.

"It will be different here. You and I are in charge of the horses now," I said.

One of the first things we did together was to

buy a brood mare. The following spring she had a chestnut foal, the first to be born at Hexham Hall for many years. We called her "Little Ginger" and she followed James wherever he went.

There was a bay gelding called Oscar that James liked to ride too. Sometimes, when our work was done, we rode to the common above Fairstowe village. James and I would race; him on Oscar and me, clinging to Beauty's neck with the wind in my long red hair. And often we would win! For although Beauty's knees were scarred, his spirt was not. He could still gallop – perhaps not as fast as he once could. But we could still beat James Howard. And, despite all my very great happiness at Hexham – with Nanny and James and the horses, and all my grand plans – I was never happier than when I was riding on Beauty's back or just standing with him under the apple trees... A horse and a girl, the very best of old friends.

> *"Joe is the best and kindest of grooms ... I shall*
> *never be sold and I have nothing to fear;*
> *and here my story ends."*
> Black Beauty *by Anna Sewell (1877)*

Author's Note

I first imagined I was riding Black Beauty when was I was eight or nine years old and reading Anna Sewell's heartbreaking classic for the very first time. I was lucky enough to live on a farm and have my very own (small, fat) pony who I rode nearly every day. Suddenly, hairy little Flora was transformed in my imagination – no longer shaggy and slow she was the sleek and speedy Black Beauty.

I did not only pretend to ride on Beauty when I was in the saddle; driving down the motorway I would stare out of the window for hours on end imagining I was leaping the hedges and fences as they flashed by in the fields beside the road. I wonder how many other children have imagined, as they stare out of the windows of city buses, rattle down country lanes in cars or pedal their bicycles across town parks, that they are riding the magnificent Black Beauty too? I wonder how many children have galloped through their imaginations since the story was first published in 1877? I wonder how many adults have? (I know I still do!)

But the gorgeousness of Beauty and those early sunny chapters of love and safety, chestnut trees and meadows, are only half the tale. There is the sadness and the suffering as well. Difficult as it was to read about the terrible treatment of cab horses in Victorian London, or to stumble, weeping, through those few painful short paragraphs of Ginger's harsh and lonely death, I loved that too. I felt the wonderful release that crying at a story can bring.

I went on to study drama many years later and learnt all about catharsis – the process of an audience releasing their own emotion while witnessing a character's suffering on stage. I knew nothing about that when I was first reading *Black Beauty*, of course. All I knew was that the chest-wrenching sobs I cried for Ginger and the other horses in Anna Sewell's hard-hitting story had real power.

Anna Sewell wanted her readers to be moved, but she wanted them to take notice too. *Black Beauty* was penned not only as a story but as a way to draw attention to the need to treat animals – and especially horses – more kindly. She makes it all too clear how harsh life could be for an animal in the changing industrial world of the 1870s. It is Anna Sewell's skill in sharing that message through the briefly glimpsed lives of her characters that has ensured *Black Beauty*'s enduring place in our hearts and on our book shelves – it sold around 100,000 copies in its first ten years and over forty million by the end of the twentieth century. Sadly, Anna Sewell died very shortly after the book was published and did not live to see any of this success for herself.

It is not only in the number of sales that we can mark the influence of this extraordinary book. Any author who ever writes an animal story – especially one about horses – must hear the distant rumble of Black Beauty's hooves. It is there in *War Horse*, Michael Morpurgo's exceptional, emotionally poignant account of a horse's view of the First World War. It is there in *Charlotte's Web*. It is there in *Babe (The Sheep Pig)* with all the little creature's trials, triumphs and tears.

I have read the story of Black Beauty many times – over and over again as a child – and several times as an adult. I noticed, when I came to it again recently after a break of a few years, that there was a hidden story there just waiting to be told. Joe Green, the poor inexperienced groom, is only mentioned twice in the original tale: once when he nearly kills Beauty by mistake and once when he finds the magnificent horse much changed at the very end of the book. I found myself beginning to wonder what happened to young Joe between page 99 and page 295. Where did he go? How had he learnt to be a "fine" groom? I found myself wondering who he really was. Where did he come from? What happened to him even before the story of Black Beauty began?

Joe started to grow in my imagination – and suddenly I knew: he wasn't Joe at all… Not Joseph Green but Josephine – a girl. That is why the young groom was so inexperienced, I decided. If he was a girl he would never have been allowed to work with horses before. After that, Joe's voice just wouldn't go away and I knew (if Anna Sewell didn't mind such liberties – which I hoped she wouldn't) that I would have to tell Joe's story and invite Black Beauty, Merrylegs and Ginger, as well as many of the other original characters, back to life to help me.

Writing *Finding Black Beauty* has been an absolute joy. Above all, working with my tireless, intelligent and funny editor Gen Herr has been a flat out, whoop-aloud gallop (with plenty of terrible horsey puns shared in emails along the way). Thanks too to all at Scholastic, especially Pete Matthews for terrier-sharp edits, and everyone in sales, marketing and design. Huge thanks as always to Claire Wilson and Pat White at RCW – a finer stable of literary agents is impossible to imagine!

My knowledge of Victorian servant life – and the stable yard in particular – was helped enormously by visits to both Audley End house in Essex and Shugborough in Staffordshire. For sense of city life at the time I found *Street Life in London* by J. Thomson and Adolphe Smith invaluable. My brother Geoffrey – never really at home in the Twentieth Century let alone the Twenty-First – was a fount of knowledge on all things Victorian (including the underwear!). Sophie McKenzie has been invaluable as always – steering the jolts and wobbles of plot like a skilled coachman on a stormy night. Huge thanks to them both and to my family too of course who have been lost in the dust blown up by Black Beauty's hooves for weeks on end. Above all I would like to thank my parents for a childhood of wide-open spaces where my imagination could gallop – this book is dedicated to them.